STONEHILL
BOOK FIVE

this old café

This is a work of fiction. Names, characters,
businesses, places, events, locales, and
incidents are either the products of the
author's imagination or used in a fictitious
manner. Any resemblance to actual persons,
living or dead, or actual events is purely
coincidental.

Cover design by Okay Creations
Book layout by Lori Colbeck

ISBN-13: 978-1-950348-12-1

STONEHILL
BOOK FIVE

this old
café

MARCI
BOLDEN

PINK SAND
— PRESS —

CHAPTER ONE

*J*enna Reid jumped back as water shot straight out of the pipe leading to her kitchen sink. She screamed, dropping the wrench when an ice-cold deluge soaked every inch of her body crammed under the industrial-sized sink. She covered the open joint with her hands but, like a fire hydrant struck by a wayward car, the stream was too powerful to be contained. Water squirted through her fingers and drenched her face.

She could have sworn she'd shut off the water, but apparently, she could add the valve to the list of things that didn't work in the broken-down kitchen of her broken-down diner. She held her breath and turned her face away as she assessed the situation, determined not to let panic set in.

She had to figure out why the valve hadn't turned off. If she didn't, she'd have to sit there holding the pipe while water sprayed her face until someone—likely her brother Marcus—came to her rescue.

She was done letting other people save her. She was an adult. A full-grown woman, damn it. She could do this. She could fix this.

She pulled herself up and shrieked, her tennis shoes skating across the wet cement flooring as she rushed toward the shut-off valve on the other side of the wide sink. She dropped to her knees and turned the handle as hard as she could. But once the valve was off, the water didn't stop. She turned the lever the other way.

Water continued flooding the cement floor.

"No," she begged. "No, no, no. Goddamn it!"

Despite her efforts, the puddle continued to grow.

The valve clearly wasn't working.

Rushing back to the sink, she slid to where she'd loosened the joint and fumbled with the pipe wrench. If she got the...*thingie-ma-jig*...tightened, maybe the water would quit spraying the entire room and she could clean up and pretend this never happened.

Then Marcus could fix it—like he'd told her *he* would. She could be grateful and repay him with dinner—like she'd told him *she* would before she decided watching a video on YouTube qualified her to be her own plumber.

The only problem—okay, not the only problem, but the biggest problem—was the pressure seemed to be increasing. The water was shooting faster. And she was certain the temperature was even colder than before. Whatever she'd done to the valve was making things worse.

A scream of frustration ripped from her as the frigid torrent made it even more difficult for her fingers to operate. Her heart pounded in her ears, nearly obscuring the constant *whishing* of water coming from the pipe. Her eyes blurred, but she wasn't sure if it was tears of defeat or water draining from her hair into her eyes. She fumbled with the pipe wrench, trying to redo what she'd undone when she'd decided to replace the section of leaking pipe, saying words that she was sure would shock most people who knew her. Jenna tended toward the innocent side of things, but she certainly had it in her to drop an F-bomb or two if the occasion called for it.

And that occasion was now, as she sat saturated on the kitchen floor of the diner that was falling down around her faster than she and her brother could duct tape it back together. She was about to let another curse rip when, without warning, the geyser turned to a trickle.

Finally, her kitchen was silent save for her desperate panting and the annoying *ping-ping-ping* that had started this entire fiasco.

The nonstop drip had been going for days. Marcus had told her what he needed to do to fix it; he'd even bought a new section of pipe and fittings. He just hadn't had the time to devote to her plumbing. Tired of hearing the sound of droplets clinking in the metal bowl she'd put under the sink, she'd decided to be her own hero.

"Way to go, genius," she muttered.

Wiping her forehead—which was pointless since her hands were as soaked as her face and the strands of dark hair sticking to it—she sat back on her heels and choked down the sob that was threatening to erupt.

"Are you okay?"

The unexpected male voice caused her to jolt. A squeal eeked out of her as she lurched back. She wobbled for a moment then landed on her ass in the pool that had formed behind her. A man emerged from the shadows on the other side of her kitchen. Her heart seemed to stop beating as she scurried back and reached for something, *anything*, she could use to protect herself.

Bowls crashed around her as she grasped a firm handle and held up...a colander. She would have laughed if it weren't for the fact that she had no other weapon within reach. Instead, she lifted the perforated bowl in warning—if he didn't back off she'd...*strain* him. "Who—who are you?"

"I was outside. Heard you scream. Thought there might be trouble." He lifted his hands as if to prove he meant no harm. "You turned off the wrong valve."

She swallowed. He spoke slowly, in a deep voice with a hint of an East Coast drawl. He wasn't from Stonehill. Just about everyone knew everyone in this small town and she didn't know him.

His skin, what she could see of it around the dark, shaggy hair, was tan from too much sun. Like he'd worked outside most of his life. The question where he was from formed in her mind but stuck in her throat. That didn't really matter at this point in time. She sat there, letting ice-cold water soak into her jeans and numb her skin as she threatened him with fine mesh.

"You turned off the valve to the faucet, but you should have turned off the main valve," he explained. "Rookie mistake."

As he came into the light, she could see that his clothes were dingy and worn. His beard was full, but not trimmed, and his hair was shiny, as if he had gone too long between washing the strands that hung over his ears.

She couldn't determine if he was homeless or just too old to pull off hipster. Either way, he'd somehow appeared in her kitchen without her noticing, and that unsettled her.

She lifted the colander when he took a full step toward her. "This may not look deadly, but I could still put your eye out with it."

He lifted his hands, again showing his innocence, and smirked behind his facial hair.

"I have no doubt that you could. But I can help. If you want. Or you can try again now that the water's off. Whichever works for you. But either way, you might want to get out of that puddle and into dry clothes. Your lips are turning blue."

Jenna finally inhaled and looked at the clothes clinging to her. If it weren't for the vintage print of Barry Manilow's face clinging to her chest, she could have just auditioned for a wet T-shirt contest. While holding a flimsy bit of steel to save herself.

What the hell was she doing? What in the actual hell did she think she was doing?

She wasn't a plumber any more than she was a business owner.

She'd been winging it for almost three years now, but she was tired. Exhausted.

And she sure as hell wasn't capable of assaulting a grown man with a strainer. If he wanted to slit her throat and rob her...

Marcus had told her a hundred times to lock the kitchen door even when she was cleaning up. He'd told her a hundred times to carry the pepper spray he'd bought for her. He'd told her a hundred times to take basic self-defense classes.

She'd done none of those.

Not only was she ill-equipped to fix her plumbing, run a business, or protect herself, but she was also freezing. A shiver ran through her as she realized just how much water her clothing and hair had absorbed.

She laughed to stop herself from crying.

When she looked up again, the stranger was standing over her. He held out a hand to help her up and she noticed the dirt caked under his nails and in his knuckles.

Homeless.

Definitely homeless.

But his gray eyes were kind. Concerned. Nothing about him felt threatening or intimidating, though Jenna was certain she should be terrified. She swallowed before accepting his help, letting him pull her to her feet, all the while hoping it wasn't a ruse to grab hold of her and drag her off.

He eased her up and immediately released his hold, taking a step back rather than running off in the night with her.

"Thank you," she said quietly.

He gestured to the pipes. "May I?"

"Please. You certainly can't do any worse than I did."

The man stepped over the puddle and kneeled to assess the mess she'd made. "I'll have this fixed before you finish mopping," he said without looking at her.

Mopping? Oh. Right. Her tennis shoes sloshed when she moved her feet. She sighed as water seeped through the mesh. After setting the strainer aside, she grabbed the rag mop and a bright yellow bucket on rollers. She watched him from the corner of her eye as she started cleaning the floor, not letting her guard down, but also fully aware that if the man decided to attack her, there wasn't much she could do about it.

She'd traded up from a strainer to a mop handle, but she wouldn't know how to use that either.

Just as she finished and squeezed as much water out of the end as she could, the man silently rose and turned on the valve at the back of the kitchen—the one that actually stopped the water flow. He went back to the sink, used his sleeve to wipe the pipe dry, and watched, as if he were waiting for something amazing to happen.

And it did. Or didn't, depending on how Jenna decided to look at it.

The incessant drip that had been making her crazy for days

didn't start. The water didn't slowly leak from the joint and form a dewdrop that would plop and echo around the room.

The man turned the valve that Jenna had tightened in her attempt to stop the water, then tested the faucet. It worked. And the dripping still didn't start.

She set the mop aside and hesitated before joining him in observing the now-dry pipe.

"This turns off the faucet," he said. "That"—he pointed to the other valve—"turns off the water *to* the faucet."

"Got it. Thanks."

He nodded. "You're welcome."

She looked him over as he wiped his hands down his dirty jeans. Just like her denim, his had absorbed a fair share of freezing water. "You're soaked."

"I'm okay. I can change."

"Where?" she asked, surprising even herself. "I mean...where were you headed?"

He didn't answer.

"For the last few weeks, whenever I've gone out to the alley, I felt like I was being watched."

"Is that why your brother put on that deadbolt that you don't use?"

Wow. He sounded just *like* her brother.

"Yeah. That's why." Her amusement faded, and she furrowed her brow at him. "How did you know my brother did that?"

His only response was, "You should use it."

"Maybe I'll start." She tilted her head. "So you're...hanging out in the alley?"

He glanced toward the sink. "You shouldn't have any more problems with that pipe."

"Would you like some coffee?" she asked as he started for the door.

He stopped. "No thanks. I'd be up all night."

"Maybe something to eat? Something...warm?"

Facing her, he took a moment to look her over. "Your lips are purple now. Go warm up before you get sick."

Jenna opened her mouth, but he disappeared through the door leading to the alley. Glancing around the kitchen, she decided she'd mopped up enough of the flood she'd caused and pushed the bucket to the back door. She paid more attention to the shadows, looking for the stranger, than to dumping the water. Her pulse quickened as she began to wonder if she was right—was there was a homeless man living in her alley? The thought put her on edge, even if he had swooped in to save her.

She went back into the kitchen and started to shut the door, but realized that would be the same as telling him she didn't trust him now that she knew he was there. That seemed rude after the way he'd helped her.

She hesitated one more moment before tugging it closed behind her, but stopped short at turning the recently installed deadbolt that he'd mentioned. After gathering up the wet towels, she dropped them in a pile to be washed the next morning—no way in hell was she dealing with that tonight—and set the tools on the shelf where Marcus liked to keep them.

Keys in hand, she turned off the lights and headed for the back door. Her heart rate picked up again. He was probably out there. Watching her. The voyeuristic homeless plumber. Going into the dimly lit alley made her uneasy, and not for the first time. If her sixth sense was correct, he'd been living out there for about five weeks now. Or at least that was when she'd first started wondering if she were being watched as she headed up the metal stairs that led to her still-under-construction second-floor apartment.

She'd tolerated the feeling for a week before mentioning it to Marcus. He'd taken a look around, but didn't find anything suspicious. No cardboard houses or piles of clothes, nothing to indicate someone was living in her alley. But she was certain now that someone was.

Jenna couldn't imagine. As soon as she'd worked up the courage to leave the fancy city loft where Peter liked to keep her, she'd never worried about not having a place to go. She'd come back to Stonehill with nothing but the clothes she could fit in a suitcase—and she was lucky to have those by the time Peter's lawyer got done with her.

Her big brother had been determined to help her start her life over. And as Jenna tended to do, she let someone else take control. She let someone else determine what she needed and how she'd get it. And even though she wasn't prepared—emotionally or financially—she let Marcus convince her she was ready to tackle her starry-eyed dream of owning a restaurant. Peter had promised her that as well, but she'd never quite managed to jump through all the hoops he required for her to get there. He had a chain of fancy restaurants in the city. The kind that served two olives and a crouton as a meal.

He'd done a guest lecture at the culinary institute when Jenna had been a student and she'd been awestruck by him. When he offered to take her under his wing and give her hands-on training, she transitioned to mesmerized. By the time he convinced her to drop out of school and become his glorified secretary—or as she liked to call herself, his *wife*—she was in over her head.

Several years passed before she started to realize her dreams were fading away because she spent all her time focusing on his. Whenever she reminded him that she had ambitions, too, he'd remind her that there was no room in San Francisco for the kind of home-style cooking she loved. The kind he said was the reason she'd had to lose twenty pounds before he'd agreed to a wedding date.

Apparently, city folk didn't need real food. Apparently, they needed more carrot roulades and toasted brioche with goat cheese on fancy platters with upmarket names only the most elite could pronounce.

And Peter needed a thinner, more contemporary version of Jenna than the one he'd asked to marry him. True to Jenna's style, she'd complied. She'd bent and wavered and lost herself in his life until she couldn't bend and waver any longer.

She'd had a dream. One Peter had promised to help her fulfill. One that was forever just out of reach because his restaurants always came first. His career always came first.

Marcus, however, delivered after one night of sipping wine at his house while complaining about how their lives hadn't quite gone as planned. Marcus had fallen head over heels for his boss, Annie, and knew she'd never return his affections as long as he worked for her, but he couldn't imagine *not* working for her. Jenna told him how she was an afterthought even before she and Peter had exchanged vows. How she'd never own a restaurant since she'd dropped out of culinary school and spent the last ten years building Peter up. She'd given him everything and received nothing.

Marcus asked if she still wanted to open a restaurant. She'd smiled and said she'd love to own a little diner, just a little place to dish up some home-style meals. The next day, he walked her through this building, telling her how they could fix it up and how she could renovate the second and third floors to be living space.

Sure, it had sounded good. It had sounded *great*. The fantasy played out well. The reality sucked.

She needed Marcus much more than either had anticipated when he handed her the keys to this old building. He fixed things almost every time he came to visit. He ate at the diner and tipped far more than he should have. He even helped her keep her budget on track since she no longer had Peter's accountants to do that for her.

For a while, Marcus didn't seem to mind. He said it made him feel useful. And one day, he let her know he finally accepted her advice and got a new job. His boss, Annie, was furious, but she came around quickly. Once they were no longer working together, they were free to date and headed for a much-deserved happily-ever-after.

But then tragedy struck and Annie nearly lost her life. Marcus spent all of his time helping her recover, and, once they were married, building a life together. Jenna didn't begrudge that. That was how marriage should have been—not like hers. She'd been treated as a burden instead of an equal. She was truly happy for her brother. But with Marcus focused on Annie, Jenna suddenly realized how ill-equipped she was to be an adult all on her own. She owned a business. But only because Marcus had backed her. She owned this run-down building. But only because Marcus had helped her buy it. She had big plans to fix it up and make it amazing. But only because Marcus had the skills to help her.

While he helped Annie, Jenna was proving how right her husband had been about her incompetence.

Jenna sniffed and shook the echo of her husband's voice from her mind.

No. She could do this. She could definitely do this.

And that cocky bastard was her *ex-husband*.

Peter didn't have a bit of control over her anymore, and she needed to stop letting him. She needed to focus on the here and now.

And right now, she needed to take that strange man's advice and get out of the cold, wet clothes that were clinging to her like a second skin. A warm shower would get the chill from her bones and a good night's sleep would help her wake up with a fresh outlook.

As she stepped out into the alley and locked the door behind her, she glanced around. Not out of fear this time, but out of guilt. Here she'd been cursing her luck over a leaking pipe and the man who helped her didn't even own a box to sleep in.

You are so selfish, Jen.

Or so Peter had told her countless times.

"Get out of my head," she muttered as she started up the stairs, determined to focus instead on how she could properly thank the man who'd come to her rescue.

sh

Daniel didn't take kindly to charity. Never had. But when he woke to a to-go cup of coffee and a Styrofoam container sitting by the dumpster with *Thank you!* scribbled across the top, he didn't turn away from the gift. Sinking down in the shadows, he looked at the café door and lifted the top off the cup. Sipping the hot brew, he closed his eyes and silently thanked the woman he assumed was responsible.

He'd heard people call her Jenna. He'd started to call her that last night when he heard her screams and assumed the worst.

He'd barged in to find her on her knees wrestling with a pipe and immediately knew she'd turned off the wrong valve.

He grinned as he remembered the curses spewing from her as she did her best to stop the water from drenching her. He'd turned off the main valve and asked if she were okay, probably scaring a dozen or so years off her life in the process. He would have apologized, but in doing so, he'd started to say her name and stopped himself. She seemed startled enough without worrying that he was stalking her.

He was in a sense. He knew her schedule. But only because he'd moved into her alley weeks before. He knew when to expect food to be dumped there. And what. Today was Tuesday. The special would be meatloaf. He *really* liked Jenna's meatloaf. She didn't fill it with chunks of bread that soaked up the grease and turned gummy. She used breadcrumbs. Like his mom used to do when he was a kid.

Daniel opened the container and found fresh eggs, bacon, sausage, and toast. He hadn't had a real breakfast for a while now. He smiled as his stomach also thanked Jenna. After scarfing down the hot meal, he gathered his sleeping bag into his go-bag and left the alley.

If today was Jenna's meatloaf day, it was also open-door day at the community center.

They welcomed anyone local, and Daniel took advantage of that. Per his routine, he signed in to the center with a fake address and headed right for the showers. After washing away several days' worth of grime, he put on shorts and a T-shirt and headed to the workout room.

As he gripped the pull-up bar, he replayed the night before through his mind. He'd watched Jenna from the shadows for weeks, but last night was the first time he'd seen her up close. Her brown eyes had widened when she'd looked up at him and she'd fallen back. Dark hair clung to her pale skin as her full lips parted. And her T-shirt...

Daniel chuckled at the image of a shaggy-haired Barry Manilow clinging to her ample chest and slight pooch of a stomach.

She'd sat there, staring up at him, and it'd taken all he had to look her in the eye. She was beautiful, and he wanted to memorize every inch of her. But he didn't have to think too much about how intimidating he'd been standing over her. If he'd given in to the urge to stare at her '70s-pop-star-clad breasts, she probably would have screamed for an entirely different reason.

After pushing through his workout, he showered again and put on what was left of his clean clothes, then headed to the room where the center offered free juice and donuts.

All of this was management's attempt at bringing in new paying clients, but Daniel had yet to be told he wasn't welcome, so he showed up every Tuesday and went through the same shower-workout-shower-eat routine.

Today, however, thanks to the breakfast Jenna had left for him, he wrapped his donut in a napkin to save for later. His stomach was full enough for now. He did down a cup of cold apple juice, though. Hiking his pack high on his back, he smiled and thanked the lady working the desk—the one who surely knew by now that he'd never sign up for a membership—and headed to the library.

Inside the cool silence, he sat at a table and looked through the help-wanted ads. He wouldn't apply for a job. But he liked to pretend that he would.

The first—and second and third—job he'd had since coming home from Afghanistan hadn't gone well.

Sadly, spending years in a war zone had left him with a few issues—issues that made it difficult to keep a job. Which made it impossible to keep his apartment. He'd get back on his feet. Somehow. Someday. He just had to get his head together first. Maybe hiding in an alley and digging in the local café's dumpster wasn't the best way to go about that, but it was what he had and he wasn't going to complain. A lot of guys had it a lot worse.

A sense of defeat washed over him, and he folded the paper. Instead of staying at the library most of the day, as he usually did on Tuesdays, Daniel headed to the laundromat. He'd found enough coins over the weekend to wash his clothes and he needed to clean the jeans he'd gotten wet and dirty while fixing Jenna's pipes.

Laundry was usually his Wednesday routine, but he didn't think routine mattered when the only thing he had to answer to was a dumpster in an alley.

CHAPTER TWO

*J*enna rubbed her hands together as yet another round of guilt tightened her gut. This time because she was lying to Marcus and she hated that. More than that, though, she'd hate the lecture he'd give her for allowing a stranger into her kitchen while no one was around to make sure she was safe. Marcus was spending far too much time examining the work the homeless man had done. Surely he was onto her by now. He must have realized someone else had done the work.

He stood up and gave her a wide smile like a proud papa seeing his kid take the first step toward adulthood. Marcus still tended to see her as the little sister he'd left behind when he headed out to see the world. Helping her find her footing after her disaster of a marriage hadn't helped squelch that image. "Nice work, Jen." He wiped his hands on a towel and then gave her a one-armed hug. "Before you know it, you'll be rewiring the outlets."

Jenna snorted. "Let's not get crazy."

He laughed softly before releasing her. Leaning against the counter, he tossed the towel aside. "I'll find time to fix that switch. Soon."

"I told you, I'll take care of it."

"I will—"

"I know. But you don't have to spend every free moment you have taking care of me."

"Maybe I want to."

"But you shouldn't have to. You have a wife now. I doubt she appreciates you spending so much time with me."

"Annie can survive without me. Trust me. She tells me that all the damn time."

Jenna imagined Annie did tell Marcus that all the time. Annie had been the epitome of independence before becoming disabled. And somehow, it seemed like she still managed to be more self-sufficient than Jenna most days. Annie might not have been able to drive, or have complete use of her hands, and it didn't take much to distract her, but she was still brilliant and Jenna had no doubt *she* would have known which valve to turn off before taking the pipes apart.

"Listen, I know you don't want to hear this, but I think we'll have to replace those pipes sooner than we anticipated," Marcus said, pulling her back to reality.

She sank physically and emotionally. "That isn't in my budget for this quarter."

"We'll look over your finances again. We need to find the money. If you don't have it—"

"I'm not taking money from you."

"Jen." He gave her that I-know-what-is-best look. "We can't keep putting duct tape on things. We need to start really fixing them. Before you get shut down."

She opened her mouth but didn't argue. She couldn't. Hard to run a restaurant with no running water. Finally she nodded. "Okay. I'll bring the books over as soon as I make sure things are okay here. You can take a look while I cook dinner."

"You don't have to—"

She shook her head to silence him. If he was going to continue to guide her through life, the least she could do was feed him and his wife. "I'll keep it simple so Annie can help."

He smiled. "She likes helping."

"I know."

Marcus kissed her head. "We'll figure it out, okay?"

"Okay. Go home. I'm sure Annie is waiting for you."

As soon as he disappeared through the swinging doors that led to the dining room, she let her forced smile fall. She'd set aside a bit of money to do some cosmetic work on the building. She'd done everything she could to not touch that money, but now she could see it slipping through her fingers and into the wallet of a plumber.

Damn it.

She grabbed the disinfecting spray, passed through the doors Marcus had left swinging, spritzed a table, and wiped it clean. Given that it was midafternoon on a workday, there was a lull in business, but she smiled at the regulars who sat at their usual tables. Bless those who came in day after day, even if they did fill tables for far longer than their meager bills and tips balanced out. Seeing their appreciative smiles made Jenna feel she was doing something right.

Never mind they were customers she had inherited when she bought out the previous owners. The little things kept her going, so she clung to them.

She stopped scrubbing a table when she realized the gunk she was trying to wash away was actually a scratch on the surface. Her frown deepened as she skimmed over the cracked vinyl booth. Most of the tables were starting to show the same wear. And the money she'd planned to use to fix them was going to end up going to new pipes.

She'd had such big plans for this place when Marcus handed her the keys, but beyond a fresh coat of paint—now three years old—she hadn't been able to do a damn thing to improve the dining area. She'd had to re-shingle the roof, patch the walls, and do some essential upgrades to the electrical. She'd also had to replace the commercial fridge and the stove. She'd had to hire more staff than expected. Not to mention the cost of supplies and utilities and every other damn thing that she had underestimated.

Every single hurdle that she had to climb felt like Peter was vindicated in his assessment of her—that she'd never be anything without him—even if he had no way of knowing her struggles to keep the café open.

"Get out of my head," she whispered, as she tended to do when his negativity clouded her. Putting her palms on the table, she noticed a man cross the street. Easing into the booth, she watched him through the window. Instead of heading down the sidewalk, he went down the alley beside the building, a green bag on his back. That must be why she'd never seen any sign of him. He must have been able to fit everything he had into that pack.

Her heart ached for him, but she remembered how lucky she was to have the problems she had. How dare she complain about bills and stretching her budget when she not only had a roof over her head, but was lucky enough to own her own business—challenging as that might have been most days.

"Hey, Sara," she called to the waitress she would leave in charge on the rare occasion that she left while the diner was open. "I need to take off early. Will you make sure to lock up at close?"

"Want me to—"

"Just lock up on your way out."

The girl always offered to clean up. Jenna wasn't sure if she was attempting to be nice or if she needed more hours on her timesheet, but Jenna couldn't afford to pay out more than she already was to her employees. She didn't mind cleaning up. In fact, she got most of her enjoyment out of the café when it was empty and she could embrace this space as her own.

She headed out through the kitchen and glanced around, but didn't see the mystery man anywhere. Deciding it would have been rude to continue staring, she went up to her apartment and grabbed what she needed to make a quick dinner for Marcus and Annie as well as her accounting notebook. Tucking it all into a tote bag, she headed to her brother's house so she could determine the best way to keep her business from going under.

sh

Daniel checked his watch again. Nearly twenty-one-hundred. The spot where Jenna usually parked her old Taurus was empty. The little red sedan only moved a few times a week, and it was always back by this time. Her lights were usually out by now.

He looked up at the window he was certain was her living room. Soft light still shined through the blue curtains.

It wasn't like her to be out this late.

She was up before the sun every single morning. Every. Day. She didn't stay out this late. Her staff hadn't even cleaned up. They'd closed the doors and walked out. Maybe because they knew something he didn't. Maybe something had happened to Jenna and they'd rushed off to check on her.

Fear for this woman he didn't even know caused his stomach to knot. He wanted to go look for her. Track her down. Confirm her status. But he didn't know where to look.

Sweat broke out on his brow. He'd been crouching, staring at her parking spot since her staff left an hour before. His thighs were on fire and his calves weren't faring much better.

The hospital was only a few blocks away. He could jog that far in minutes. But asking if *Jenna who owns the café* had been admitted wasn't likely to get him an answer.

Marcus.

Her brother's name was Marcus. And her sister-in-law was Annie. That was the extent of what he knew about her. He checked his watch again—21:06.

He finally pulled his focus from her parking spot to the café. After glancing around one more time, he went to the door that led to her kitchen. She rarely locked the deadbolt, but he'd heard the click before her waitresses left. He didn't have the tools to pick the lock, but he was certain he could find a way into the building. Maybe one of her staff had left a hint to where Jenna had gone.

He tried the back door first, just in case. As he suspected, the lock had been turned. He examined the door. It wasn't the sturdiest thing he'd seen, but he didn't want to damage Jenna's property. He moved to the back of the building and checked the window that looked into the kitchen. He frowned when he noticed the lock. *Lock* was a very loose term for what was supposedly keeping Jenna safe. He didn't even have to take the combat knife from the sheath hooked to his jeans to pry the window open. The flimsy-ass latch was about as secure as just leaving the damn door open, as she had the previous night.

After popping the screen off, he pressed his hand firmly to

the pane and moved the frame up and down, up and down, up and down—watching as the lock jerked with the movement. Up and down. Up and down. And *pop*. The lock released, and Daniel slid the window open. Nothing to it.

Her brother really needed to work on the security if his sister was going to own, operate, and freaking *live* in this building. She was an easy target for any thug with half a brain and an ounce of ambition. Hefting himself up, Daniel climbed through the window and silently landed in the kitchen.

He immediately scanned the dimly lit room before pulling a compact LED flashlight from his pocket. He sighed at the sink full of dishes and the pile of pots and pans on the stove. These kids didn't give a damn about her or her business. He looked at the board with notes and schedules, but found no indication of where Jenna might be. He stepped closer, searching for a number for Marcus.

He had no idea what he'd say to the man. *I'm a stranger just checking in on your sister.* But that would be better than not knowing. If something happened to Jenna, there wasn't a damn thing he could do about it. But he needed to know. Not knowing wasn't an option.

Easing into the dining room, he found more mess. The floor hadn't been swept. Tables hadn't been wiped. Lowering his flashlight, Daniel exhaled with a sense of frustration. He'd seen how hard she worked. He'd seen how exhausted she was climbing the stairs at night, only to get up before the sun to do it again. She deserved better than this, damn it.

Skimming the light over the tables again, he decided that if he couldn't find Jenna, the least he could do was leave her with one less thing to deal with. Going from window to window, he lowered and closed the blinds. He wouldn't turn on the overhead lights, but with the blinds drawn, anyone walking by would be less likely to notice any kind of movement from his flashlight.

Once he was safe behind the shades, he went to the closet where she'd put her cleaning supplies the night before. The beam from his flashlight wasn't much, but it was enough as he went to work on wiping down the tables. As soon as all the remaining crumbs had been knocked to the floor, he swept up the food bits and discarded straw wrappers.

A quick once-over with the broom, and he bent to gather the pile of debris into the dustpan. He'd just squatted when a noise behind him drew his attention. Shit. He'd been so caught up in cursing her staff that he hadn't been paying attention to his surroundings.

Who's making goddamn rookie mistakes now, Colonel?

He was plotting all the ways to defend himself when the light flipped on overhead.

"What the...?" Jenna asked from behind him. Her question was clipped. Irritated.

He turned slowly on his heels, still crouched with the broom and dustpan in his hands. She had a small black canister held out in front of her and he couldn't help but grin.

"Pepper spray is significantly more effective than a strainer, but still not as intimidating as a gun."

She lowered her hand and sighed. "You sound like my brother."

"If I were your brother, you'd have better locks on this building."

She creased her brow as she looked at what he was doing. "You broke in to clean?"

"Your staff left a mess."

"I told them to."

"Why?"

"Because I'd rather lose a few hours of sleep cleaning up myself than have to pay out more than I can afford for them to do it. You actually broke into my café to clean?" she repeated. "I could have you arrested."

The relief he had at seeing her standing there, perplexed by his actions but safe, wasn't something he understood. Or wanted to try to understand. He felt responsible for her somehow. Like eating out of her dumpster made him obligated to protect her from a world she didn't seem to recognize was dangerous. She left her door open, walked a dimly lit flight of stairs every night, sometimes carrying a moneybag, and had just walked in on an intruder with nothing more than a can of pepper spray. She was a target and she didn't even know it.

"I was worried about you," he admitted.

"Worried about me?"

He nodded as he stood. "In the last five weeks, you've never once been gone this late."

She tensed again. "You...you know my schedule?"

"Your routine is predictable. That's not safe."

"Hard to alter my routine when I literally live a flight of stairs away."

"And you shouldn't carry money with you at night. Keep it in a safe until morning."

Fear lit in her eyes.

"I'm not going to rob you. Never crossed my mind. But that doesn't mean someone else wouldn't. And you're making it too easy for them."

She drew a deep breath and let it out slowly. "Look, I don't want any trouble from you."

"And you won't get any."

"Is this the first time you've done this?"

"Yes, ma'am. I was hoping to find a way to contact your brother. To let him know you hadn't come home."

She lifted her chin a notch. "I was with my brother. Not that I owe you an explanation."

Daniel nodded. It wasn't like he didn't know his panic was foolish. He just couldn't always control his impulse to protect. "You're right. You could have me arrested. Or you could let me make it up to you."

"How so?"

"Community service for my misdeed. Your kitchen is a disaster. It's late. You're usually in bed by now."

She tensed again.

"I wait for all your lights to go out before I open the dumpster."

"Look... I don't know you. I'm not going to leave you here unsupervised. The fact that you got in here is unsettling enough. I'm not going to pretend I didn't just catch you..."

He looked at the dustpan in his hand. "Cleaning."

She shook her head and creased her brow as her voice rose several octaves. "Why are you cleaning?"

"I thought... If something happened to you, you shouldn't have to come back to a mess."

She stared at him, clearly not sure what to say. Finally she asked, "How did you get in?"

"Back window."

Her eyes widened. "You broke—"

"I didn't break anything. Those locks are flimsy and easy to open. If you can't afford better windows, you should at least put bars in the tracks to stop them from sliding open."

"That could be a code violation."

"Only if you use it during business hours. You won't be blocking an exit. Just securing a window."

She narrowed her eyes at him. "You know commercial building code off the top of your head?"

He smirked. "Some."

"Who are you?"

His amusement faded. "Nobody. I'm nobody. I'm sorry about breaking into your place. It won't happen again."

She stepped to the side, blocking his way before he could get to the kitchen. "I'm Jenna Reid."

"Jenna," he said just above a whisper. He'd thought her name a hundred times, but this was the first time he'd spoken it. Somehow the word felt right on his lips.

"And you are?"

"Daniel," he said after a few moments of consideration.

"Daniel?"

"Maguire."

"You know how to use a mop, Daniel Maguire?"

CHAPTER THREE

*J*enna glanced over her shoulder as she loaded another rack of dishes to run through the industrial dishwasher. While she appreciated the speed of the machine, she wasn't particularly keen on the noise level. Daniel could have sneaked up on her any time during the two-minute cycle, and she wouldn't have heard him coming. She should have told him to leave. She should have called the police. She should have called Marcus and told him how easy it was to break into the café.

"Stupid," she muttered as she closed the door.

"What's stupid?"

She squealed and faced him. "Would you *please* stop sneaking up on me?"

"Sorry."

He actually did look contrite as he leaned on the mop. "The dining room is done."

"Thank you."

She didn't have to ask him; he pushed the mop bucket to the back door and dumped the water. While she didn't appreciate finding him in her dining room, it was nice to have help cleaning up. Especially after coming home later than she'd expected. She and Annie had cooked a nice dinner while Marcus pored over her books. Then, over spaghetti and garlic bread, he told her that despite her intentions, she would definitely have to dip into the money she'd set aside for the dining room if she wanted to fix the plumbing properly.

Perfect. She'd have running water, but the dining room would be so run-down nobody would want to eat there anyway. She ground a scrubber against the counter, taking out some of her aggression as she ran Marcus's next suggestion through her head.

"Maybe it's time, Jen. Get out while you can."

He was right. She knew he was right. If she kept dumping money into this place, she was going to end up in debt so deep she'd never find her way out. Biting her lip, she tried to keep tears at bay. She hated giving up but he was right. As always.

She gasped softly when the squeak of tiny plastic wheels pulled her from her thoughts. Glancing back at the homeless man returning the mop bucket to its place, she wondered if she should ask him for pointers on how to survive on the streets. Maybe they could hang out in the alley together. She laughed flatly at the image.

Marcus would never let her be homeless. She'd end up living

in his and Annie's basement and they'd all pretend that her cooking and cleaning and helping Annie was payment enough.

Turning, Jenna leaned against the counter and sighed. "I have to close the café."

"Yes. It's late."

"No. I mean... The reason I was out late is because my brother and I were going over my budget. The pipes need to be replaced. Apparently so do the window locks. There are electrical issues I can't keep ignoring. I set aside some money to update the dining area but it's not enough. I can't do everything and keep my nose above water, but if I don't do everything I'll never make enough revenue to keep my nose above water anyway. I...I have to get out before I drown. My brother is a real estate agent. He got me a great deal on this place and with the minor improvements I've made, he can probably get me enough to break even. Or close enough that the difference doesn't sink me." She looked at the man who stood silently staring at her. "Sorry. I don't mean to dump my problems on you. You have your own issues to sort out. Thanks for helping tonight. Not for, you know, committing a misdemeanor, but for cleaning the dining room. And for worrying about me. That was nice of you."

"Where will you go?"

She shrugged. "Doesn't really matter, does it? I can't keep butting my head against these walls. They're crumbling faster than I can patch them." She walked to the fridge and scanned the contents before taking out a bowl of leftover chicken salad.

He looked at her offering before shaking his head. "I don't want handouts. I'll work for what I take or eat from the trash."

"You cleaned my dining room."

"I owed you that for breaking in."

She pushed the bowl toward him again. "It will probably end up in the dumpster anyway. Might as well eat it before the risk of food poisoning increases. Take it."

He hesitated before accepting the food. "Thanks."

"I've got the rest of this. I appreciate your help, Daniel."

He offered her a weak smile. "I appreciate not spending the night in jail, Jenna." He stopped at the door. "Lock this behind me. Please."

She nodded and he disappeared, and then she did as he requested and turned the deadbolt. She took a few minutes to switch the load in the dishwasher, and while the last pans were being washed, she walked through the dining room. Daniel had done a good job of cleaning. He'd even made sure all the napkin dispensers and salt and pepper shakers were centered, just as she did every night.

A feeling washed over her. Not fear, as she suspected she should've felt. Clearly he'd been watching her. Keeping tabs on her routine right down to how she set the tables each night. But she didn't feel threatened by that stalker-esque behavior, as she probably should have. She wasn't even angry that he'd broken into the café. He hadn't done any damage. She'd checked the window as she closed and re-locked it. Other than a greasy handprint on the outside, there was no sign Daniel had come in that way.

The thought that someone else could break in just as easily set her more on edge than the man who had actually done it. Something deep in her gut trusted him, though he'd given her no reason to. Well, no reason beyond the fact that he'd been living outside her building for over a month and had plenty of opportunities to mug, rape, and-slash-or murder her and had done none of the above.

He had seemed genuinely concerned about her. He'd swept her floor so that she wouldn't have to come back to a mess? The only other person she could think of who would ever be so considerate toward her was her brother. Marcus was always doing little things like that to help her out. He hadn't always, but he had turned into a mother hen. Since Annie hated it, he tended to expel that energy on Jenna. She hated it too, but far less than his wife. Jenna wasn't nearly as assertive as her sister-in-law. Annie didn't just tell Marcus to stop taking care of her; she *made* him stop. Jenna didn't. She let Marcus be Marcus and it seemed to suit them both.

His voice echoed through her mind as she looked around the space she'd worked so hard to make her own.

"Maybe it's time, Jen. Get out while you can."

Reaching behind the counter, where she kept extra cash-register tape, napkins, and other things she might need on the fly, Jenna pulled out a binder. Every time she saw something in a magazine or online that she wanted to do to the café, she stuck a copy of the photo in the file. She'd wanted to restore the diner to its original glory. She had framed photos of the old café hanging behind the counter, but decades of updates and new owners trying to modernize the business had taken much of the charm away. She wanted to restore it. Bring it back.

But the cracked vinyl booths, torn linoleum flooring, and twenty-year-old paneling wasn't going to be replaced on her watch. Maybe the next owner would have better luck.

Heaving a sigh, Jenna slammed the binder closed, tossed the book in the trash behind the counter, and headed home.

Daniel hadn't slept the night before. And it wasn't because he was hiding in the shadows with nothing more than his sleeping bag for comfort. He'd had plenty of nights like that over the years. He kept thinking about the look in Jenna's eyes as she told him she was going to sell the café. She'd been heartbroken. But he had to admire her for getting out while she still could. Too many business owners held on too long. She had to sell the place while she still had something to fall back on.

But he hated it for her. She seemed like a good person. One of those people who actually cared about other people, even when it didn't benefit them. He'd seen her with her customers. Elderly, disabled, poor...homeless and living in her alley...she didn't seem to see them for that. If she did, she didn't treat them differently than anyone else.

She never looked at him like he deserved to be where he was. Like if he just tried harder to get a job, he wouldn't be eating out of the trash. He'd had a job. He'd had plenty of jobs. He just...

He couldn't keep them. Not now. Not until he got his head straight.

Running his hand over his face, he exhaled loudly. Today was Wednesday, if he remembered correctly. His usual laundry day, but since he'd done that yesterday, he had a full day to do nothing but bum around—literally. He could go to the library. Find a book to read instead of looking at want ads he wouldn't reply to. He used to enjoy reading.

He was clipping the clasp on his bag closed when the door to the café opened. Though Jenna had gone to work almost two hours ago, for some reason he expected her to be walking out, smiling brightly at him. But it was the kid who worked in the kitchen. Daniel wasn't fond of him. He hadn't done anything wrong; he just didn't have the best work ethic. He'd sit on the back steps during his break and talk on his phone, smoking and bitching about cleaning grease traps while Jenna chatted with the customers or complaining that he hadn't had a raise in the entire year he'd worked there.

Daniel could see why. The kid didn't seem too inclined to go above and beyond to help anyone. That was proven yet again when he flipped the top of the dumpster open and tossed a bag of trash in but didn't bother closing the lid. Jenna always closed the lid. Always.

As soon as he was alone in the alley again, Daniel hoisted his backpack onto his shoulders and grabbed the lid to flip it closed. Through the thin white plastic of the bag, he noticed a book with bold writing across the front. *Café Plans.*

He glanced at the kitchen door before reaching in and grabbing the bag. He pulled it open, tugged the binder free, and looked at a few pages. Pictures of booths. Décor. Tabletops.

Café Plans. Jenna's plans. Tossed in the trash.

Daniel again recalled the sadness in her eyes the night before. She'd given up.

Looking at the closed door—the one he'd watched her go through for the last few weeks—he held his breath, debating.

No. She wasn't giving up. He wouldn't let her. Not without a fight.

Tucking the book under his arm, Daniel closed the dumpster and headed to the library. The women there didn't seem to mind him visiting several times a week. They didn't seem to notice him, actually. He hoped that if he kept a low profile, that trend would continue. When he arrived, he found a table far from the aisles of books and opened the binder.

There were far too many ideas to do them all—her café would end up looking like a flea market—but Daniel could see how some of her pictures would work together. Grabbing a pencil and paper from the center of the table, presumably for library visitors to jot research down, Daniel made a list. Jenna had mentioned that the pipes needed replacing and that there was electrical work to be done. Those were must-haves. He also wanted her to have stops on the windows so no one else could get into the café as easily as he had. Blocks of wood placed on the tracks each night at closing would do for now, but eventually he'd install better locks.

The must-haves for the dining room would be more challenging. She needed to reupholster the booths. The paneling was old and cracked in places; that needed updating as well. Paint was easy. She just needed a fresh coat, something that would stand up a bit better than whatever she'd used before. The scratches in the veneered tabletops could be fixed for now, but eventually she'd want to upgrade to something nicer.

The flooring was his main concern. The tiles she had a picture of would get expensive fast. He wondered how she'd feel about going with concrete. He could tear the floor out and have it repaired in a matter of days. She wouldn't lose much business. Unless the flooring underneath was cracked or there were foundation problems. Always a possibility in a building that old, and something he couldn't know until he'd already damaged her floors beyond repair.

Maybe tiles were better. He'd have to think on that.

He needed measurements of the café. He needed the dimensions of the floor and of the booths and tables. He closed his eyes and counted from memory how many stools, booths, and tables lined the café, but he had no way of confirming any of the sizes.

Looking at his list, he debated where to start.

sh

Jenna glanced up at the sound of knuckles rapping on the back door. "Oh, you do know how to knock."

Daniel smiled. "Yes, ma'am."

"Ugh. Don't call me ma'am. I hear that all day long and it makes me feel so old."

"Yes. Jenna. I thought maybe…if you need help."

She didn't. She'd been doing this on her own for three years, but she gestured toward the closet where she kept cleaning supplies. "Feel free." He seemed to need to sweep her dining room more than she needed him to. He disappeared through the swinging doors with a broom, and she went back to the dishes. She had just finished filling the mop bucket, wondering what was taking him so long, when he came back. He didn't say a word, just handed her the broom and took the mop to the dining room.

She followed him out this time, though. As soon as she stepped into the dining room, she wrinkled her nose as a metallic scent assaulted her. "What is that smell?"

He didn't look up from the floor he was cleaning. "Lacquer."

"Lacquer?"

"To fix the scratches in the table."

Creasing her brow, she walked to the closest table and looked to the spot where someone had obviously dragged a fork along the surface with malicious intent. The scrapes were gone and replaced with a sheen she hadn't seen on the table since —ever.

"Don't touch," he warned before her fingers could brush over the surface. "It'll take a few hours to dry completely."

"How did you—"

"Wood filler and lacquer."

A sense of unease rose in her chest. "You carry wood filler and lacquer around in your backpack? Daniel?" she pressed when he didn't answer.

He finally stopped running the mop over the floor. "I didn't steal if that's what you were thinking. I found a dented can of lacquer in the trash behind Carson's Hardware. I had enough cash to buy the filler. It's only a few bucks for a fill stick. Just because I'm down on my luck doesn't mean I'm a thief."

She lowered her gaze, ashamed that her first instinct had been that he'd stolen the supplies. "Not every business owner around here will ignore someone going through their trash. I don't want you getting in trouble to help me."

"That stuff's just going to the landfill anyway."

"Even so. You could be arrested if the owner pressed charges. Please don't do that again."

He stared at her for a moment before nodding.

She looked at the table again. "You did an amazing job."

"I only had enough lacquer to do the first row of tables. I'll do the rest another time."

"Thank you."

"You're welcome."

He went back to cleaning, and she watched for a few moments before going in search of some dinner to give in exchange for his work. When he joined her, she pulled a plate from the microwave and set it on the counter with a glass of milk.

"Don't argue," she said when he opened his mouth, clearly to protest. "Wash first," she instructed, and went back to wiping the kitchen down.

He cleaned his hands and face and then ate in silence. When he was done, he went to the sink and washed his dishes and then set them aside. She'd run them through the dishwasher before using them for customers, but his intention was appreciated.

CHAPTER FOUR

*D*aniel took a deep breath before approaching the construction site. Several men looked up; a few muttered in disbelief, while others let their conversations fall quiet as he passed. He ignored them all. He was there to see the foreman.

Charlie Burke frowned when his gaze locked on Daniel's. "Danny," he started.

"I'm not here for a job," he was quick to say. "I have one."

His uncle glanced away for a moment, but not before Daniel saw the relief in his eyes. "Good. I'm glad. I've been worried about you."

"I told you not to," he said with a slight grin. "I might not be fully adjusted to civilian life, but I do know how to take care of myself."

"Where are you staying?"

"With a friend."

Charlie shook his head. He always knew when Daniel was lying. As a kid, Daniel had tried to steal a beer from the fridge and blame it on his older cousin. Despite his best efforts and most convincing story, Charlie had seen through him.

"What friend?" his uncle asked.

"Her name is Jenna. I'm doing some work for her."

"A woman friend?"

"Yeah. Does that matter?"

Charlie sighed and Daniel didn't need to ask why. The apple hadn't fallen far from the tree in a lot of ways, but Daniel wasn't a conman like his dad. Despite what his uncle thought.

"What do you need, kid?"

"Tools. A truck."

"I don't have any—"

"After hours, Charlie. Just let me use some of your stuff after hours. You know I'll take care of it."

"Yeah, I know." He exhaled loudly. "Come home with me. Shower. Shave. You look like shit. And you don't smell much better."

"Your wife isn't comfortable with me in her house, Charlie."

"She's at work."

He shook his head. "She doesn't want me in her house. I'll respect her wishes."

Charlie heaved another of those sighs. He felt guilty, but Daniel didn't blame Lisa. Daniel reacted on instinct. His instinct had saved him a hundred times—hell, a *thousand* times—while he was in the army. But he wasn't in the army now and those instincts just didn't fit into the real world well. He had frightened his uncle's second wife more than once while staying with them. When he'd gotten into a fight on Charlie's worksite, she told his uncle she didn't trust Daniel to be in their house.

Daniel didn't want her to fear him. He didn't want her to be uncomfortable in her own home. So he left. And he quit his uncle's construction crew. And he moved into an alley to figure out his next move. And while he worked that out, he'd put his skills to good use and would help Jenna.

He hadn't asked for the hot meal she'd offered last night, but he hadn't turned it down either. She felt like he'd earned it, so he'd taken it. He wasn't sure if this was going to be an acceptable practice for her, but until she told him otherwise, he planned to help her out. And if he got a hot meal or two in return, he wouldn't complain.

She didn't want to sell her café but she couldn't keep it if she didn't make the necessary improvements. Daniel might not have been able to do much about his situation, but he could help with hers. She was hurting and for some reason he felt compelled to help. Maybe because it gave him purpose or because she didn't look at him with pity or...or because she seemed as lost as he felt. Whatever the reason, so long as she let him, he'd help her. But in order to do that, he had to come crawling to his uncle.

"I'll have everything back to you before morning," he promised.

"Tools and the truck. For how long?"

"A couple weeks. She has a few larger projects that I can't do without a truck."

Charlie nodded. "Okay. Just... Don't start no trouble with her, Danny."

"I'm not out to start any trouble, Charlie."

Daniel hesitated. He wasn't one to ask for favors, but since he was already here, he thought he should just go all in. Jenna didn't want him searching through trash bins to help her fix up her café, and he understood her concern even if he didn't agree with it. It usually took more for him to tarnish his pride like this, but Jenna deserved it and he was certain he could make things even with his uncle eventually. He'd barter some work for him down the road.

"What else do you need?" Charlie asked flatly.

"I'm a bit low on cash right now. I'm not asking for money, but...got any scraps I can sort through? Maybe some leftover paint?"

"Boy," he said with a sigh, "you're lucky I promised your mama I'd look out for you."

That promise had been made to Charlie's dying sister thirty years ago. Daniel hadn't called upon it since joining the army twenty-five years prior, but when he'd come home and didn't know what to do or where to go, he'd reached out to his uncle and asked for the help he'd always been too proud to lean on. He just wished he hadn't screwed up so badly. Maybe helping Jenna would do more than let her save her café and give Daniel something to fill his time. Maybe he'd finally show Charlie that he wasn't like the father who'd been nothing more than a common crook.

As six a.m. neared, Jenna walked into the café and inhaled. She exhaled, and inhaled again. "Oh, god," she moaned as a distinct chemical smell filled her nostrils. She immediately thought of gas. She had a gas leak. The entire building was going to catch and blow up and she'd be up to her eyeballs in insurance claims. Actually, come to think of it, that was probably better than being up to her eyeballs in debt.

Marcus was planning to drop by sometime today with suggestions on a selling price so he could get the ball rolling on putting the café on the market. Her heart ached at the thought, but she had to admit the idea of not standing on a cliff looking down at nothing but bankruptcy would be a blessing.

Sniffing the air, she pushed the door open to the dining room and gasped. Fresh paint. The smell filling the café was paint. The wall by the front door and the one stretching behind the countertop along one side of the café was coated in crisp, clean, freshly painted white.

"Daniel," she whispered.

She headed straight to the alley and found the culprit sleeping behind the dumpster. "Daniel? Hey. Daniel."

His eyes shot open and he looked up at her.

She frowned at the streak of dried paint down the front of his jeans. "You painted the café?"

He grunted as he tried to sit up. Reaching down, she grabbed his arm and tugged until he leaned against the wall, looking exhausted. She crouched down and waited until he finished yawning and met her gaze again. His gray eyes were bloodshot and had bags big enough to carry whatever was stuffed in his backpack.

"You painted the café."

"Yes, ma'am...Jenna."

"Why?"

He didn't respond and she sighed, trying not to let her frustration show.

"Daniel. Why did you paint my café?"

"You wanted it painted."

Disconcerted by his answer, she hesitated in asking, "How do you know what I want?"

He stared at her for a good five seconds before reaching into his bag. He pulled out an inch-wide three-ring binder and flipped to a page.

She not only recognized the image but knew the list by heart. The first item written in her messy penmanship was repainting the café walls white. She stared at the crossed-off item as her lips fell into a deep frown. "Come with me."

Standing, she waited as he moved slowly, stiffly, gathering his belongings. Once his sleeping bag was in his pack, which he clipped closed, he stood and followed her inside.

"Set your bag down and wash," she instructed. As he did, she turned on the griddle and dug eggs and bacon out of the fridge.

"What day is it?" he asked.

"Friday." She moved on to start a pot of coffee. "I'd say TGIF, but since I work seven days a week, I don't see the thrill in it."

"Since I don't work any day of the week, *I* don't see the thrill in it." He splashed water over his face and patted himself dry with some paper towels.

Leaning her hip against the counter, she crossed her arms and waited until he faced her. "I want to thank you, Daniel, but I'm sure you can understand I'm a bit concerned. Where did you get the paint?"

"A friend."

"A friend?"

He stared at her. "My uncle."

"Your uncle?"

He also leaned against the counter. "He owns a construction company. I went to see him yesterday and asked if he had any extra paint. He had about half of a five-gallon bucket. Sure, he could have used it on another project, but he gave it to me. Guilt."

"Guilt?"

He tossed the wadded-up paper towels into the trash. "Are you going to repeat everything I say?"

"Probably. At least until I understand what's going on."

"I was crashing at his place for a while. His wife didn't want me there. So I left. Now I'm crashing in your alley."

One piece of the mystery solved. "Why didn't she want you there?"

"She found me intimidating."

His confession was a big red flag that she would be stupid to ignore. If his own aunt was scared of him, Jenna certainly should have been. But in true Jenna the Naïve fashion, she merely took a mental note of the warning and pressed on. "Why would she be intimidated by you?"

"I just left active duty. It's hard trying to adjust to living in a world where people aren't trying to kill you all the time. I can be jumpy. Confrontational at times. I made her nervous."

More red flags. But Jenna just couldn't see what he was describing. This man seemed guarded but kind. Sure, he'd broken the law more than once, but both times was to help her out. What was she going to hold against him? The cleaning or the painting? Maybe his attempt to check on her when no one else in the world would have even noticed she was missing.

He might not have had the best approach, but his intentions seemed honorable.

Of course, that was the way of thinking that got her into such a mess with Peter. *He means well.* She'd told her friends and brother that a thousand times. Finally, even she couldn't believe her own lies and she'd had to face the fact that she'd been used. For ten solid years, she'd been a steppingstone for her husband, and once he got high enough, he didn't even bother stepping on her face any longer. He just pretended she didn't exist.

Here was another man doing insane things and telling her it was for her own good. And she was believing him. She really was a fool. She should've been shooing him out the door and calling the police to have him forced from her alley. However, the paint streak on his jeans reminded her that she at least owed him breakfast before shunning him.

"Clearly there's more to this story," she said. "I'd like to hear it."

He finally noticed the stain on his pants and scratched at it to no avail; the paint was already set into the fabric. "I found a job when I got back. This punk-ass kid wasn't pulling his weight and spent more time talking shit to his superiors than doing his job. That doesn't fly in the army, so I called him on it. He pushed. I pushed back harder."

"You got fired."

He nodded. "From that job and the next one. After that, I called my uncle. I thought being near family would help me with the transition. We were never close, but he gave me a guest room and a job on his construction crew. He and his wife tried to make me feel welcome but I'd told him about my trouble and it was obvious he'd told her. She always looked at me like she was just waiting for me to snap. Then one day I did. I heard a guy on his crew bragging about how he had to smack his wife around to get her in line. I pushed first and hardest that time. It was what she needed to prove to my uncle I shouldn't be there." He sighed and shrugged. "Looks like I'm not cut out for civilian life anymore."

"The VA has programs—"

"I can take care of myself. I'll get on my feet. I just need some time to rewire my way of thinking. I'll get there."

Smelling the heated oil from the griddle, Jenna refocused on cooking. "Pour us some coffee, please."

"How do you take it?"

"Black is fine." She dropped several slices of bacon on the surface and then faced him again as the meat started to sizzle. "So you need time to adjust. Then what are you going to do? Will your uncle give you a job again?"

He held out a cup to her, which she gratefully accepted. "My uncle Charlie's a good guy. He's my mom's brother. She died when I was a kid."

"I'm sorry."

He continued as if she hadn't spoken. "We stayed in touch from time to time, but I hadn't seen him for a few years. My dad spent more time planning get-rich-quick schemes than working. Even though Charlie was here and we were in Atlantic City, he was always there to help out if I needed him. I knew Dad wouldn't send me to college, so I joined the army. Was closing in on twenty-five years."

"And?"

He looked down, and she suspected what he was going to say.

"I got in a fight. Dishonorable discharge. Career ruined. Pension gone. No VA benefits. Not that I'd take them when there are guys hurting a lot more than I am."

She frowned. "I see a pattern emerging, Daniel."

He sipped his coffee instead of responding, so she refocused on the griddle.

"How do you want your eggs?"

"Fresh and hot. Anything beyond that is a luxury right now."

She cracked several eggs to fry them and flipped the bacon before heaving a sigh. "Should I be scared of you?"

"I have a trigger. I doubt you'd ever trip it."

"Seems wise to avoid that. What's your trigger?"

He rolled his shoulders. She was clearly making him uncomfortable, but she wasn't exactly enjoying the turn her morning had taken. She hadn't expected to find the vagabond from her alley had done improvements on her café before admitting he had a temper so bad he couldn't hold a job. She looked at him when he didn't answer, silently pushing for more information.

"My dad wasn't a nice guy. I was a kid who couldn't do much to protect my mom. I'm not a kid anymore. If I see a man hurting a woman, I tend to react before thinking. Unless you have an abusive side I haven't seen, I doubt you'd see my temper flare."

"Is that what got you discharged? You saw a man hurting a woman?"

He looked into his mug. "She was a refugee seeking the safety we were supposed to be providing. She was fleeing that kind of treatment. Not looking for it."

"You were protecting her?"

"Yes. But it wasn't my place."

She furrowed her forehead as she tried to process his words. "What do you mean? Why wouldn't that be your place? Isn't that what you were there to do?"

"He wasn't an American soldier. I should have turned a blind eye to keep the peace. Or so I was told."

She again stared, digesting what he'd said. "The army would have you turn your back on someone being assaulted?"

"The politics of war are still politics, Jenna. The man I attacked wasn't just a soldier. He was a colonel of the Afghan Army. I screwed up the balance, and they made an example out of me. I was planning on retiring from the army at a very old age. Or dying on the ground. I fit there. My...attitude...is what it takes to live in that world. Unfortunately, it gets me in trouble in this one."

She laughed softly. "As it should. You can't go around beating people up."

He nodded. "Yeah, I've figured that out."

Frowning, she changed the direction of the conversation. "Why are you helping me?"

"Why wouldn't I?"

She tilted her head and lifted her brows, once again pushing for an answer with just the look on her face.

He set his cup aside. "You seem nice. You work hard. I know your brother tries to help you out, but I've heard you talking about how his wife needs him more. Seems like you could use a break that doesn't look to be coming. Thought I'd try to make things easier for you."

"That's all. Just a homeless army vet breaking into my building in the middle of the night to make things easier for me?"

He seemed to debate with himself before shrugging. "If this place is fixed up and it doesn't cost you a fortune, you can keep it. You won't have to sell out. I know you don't want to. I saw in your eyes that you don't want to."

"No," she said softly. "I don't. But…I don't know anything about you, Daniel. Other than you apparently have a problem controlling your temper and that you've broken into my building at least twice. If I had any sense at all, that would be enough for me to send you packing. Who breaks into a building to clean and do repairs?"

"Just homeless army vets."

She didn't want to, but she chuckled at his joke. "Look, the problems with this café are deeper than scratched tables and chipped paint. That's just aesthetics. I need real work done—plumbing and electrical."

"That's nothing I can't handle."

"But are you even qualified to handle that?"

"Yes. I am. I wouldn't do anything I wasn't qualified to do, Jenna."

She bit her lip, gnawing as she contemplated. "Why does this old café even matter to you?"

"I like your cooking. Even if you are burning the eggs."

She examined the now-firm circles. Not burned. Just more done than usual. "Nobody works that hard for nothing. What's in it for you?"

Silence stretched while she filled two plates.

Finally, he said, "You need help. I need a project to keep me sane until I know what my next step is."

She carried their plates to a table and he followed with two mugs of coffee. "So your uncle gave you paint because he feels guilty that your aunt kicked you out—"

"I left because I made her uncomfortable."

"Okay. You left and your uncle feels guilty. So he gave you paint for my café?"

"He gave me paint to repay the friend I told him was helping me out."

She set their plates on a table. "And exactly how am I helping you?"

"I would have starved to death by now if it weren't for your dumpster."

"That's not quite the same as *helping* you." She slid into a booth, but he stood, staring down at his plate. "Something wrong?"

He slowly met her gaze. "I can't remember the last time I sat down with someone and ate breakfast at a table."

"Well. Maybe it's time to change that. Sit."

He eased into the booth and inhaled the scents of bacon and eggs wafting to him from a plate. Which sat next to a knife and fork. Funny how something so simple could be so damn humbling.

"I don't want you breaking into my café, Daniel."

"You should have a security system."

She frowned. "I have cameras to appease my insurance agent, but a monitored system is expensive. I can't afford that right now."

"At least put better locks on the windows."

She used the side of her fork to cut her egg. "How many times have you broken in?"

"Just to check on you and to paint."

"Do you know how bizarre that is? To break into a diner, not to eat or seek shelter, but to check on me and to paint the walls?"

"I already told you I'm not a thief. There's plenty of food in the dumpster and I've slept in far worse conditions than your alley. I had no reason to break in."

"But someone else could." She frowned as he nodded. "What would it take to fix the locks?"

"New locks and a couple hours."

"And you could do that?" She bit her lip when he nodded. "How much would it cost me?"

"I'll go to the hardware store today and see what they have and get an estimate."

"What would it cost me for you to do it?"

He looked at his plate. "Dinner."

After taking a few moments to consider his offer, she said, "Deal."

CHAPTER FIVE

"*Y*ou painted," Marcus said, his voice likely as confused as Jenna's had been when she realized what had been done to the diner.

She looked up at the wall. "Well. Someone else painted, actually."

"Good. That's good. Any little thing you can do will help with the sale price."

She sat across from him as he dropped into his usual booth. She had been hesitant to get on board with Daniel's desire to fix up the café, but after she agreed to let him fix the locks, he told her how easy it would be to replace the chipped and cracked paneling with the wainscoting she had pictured in her book. And he could replace the vinyl on the booths and stools.

One month. He could have her café dining room fixed up in one month. Then he could dig into the larger plumbing and electrical issues she'd been putting off.

He asked her to give him one month to make a few changes to the dining area, and then she could reevaluate things. If she still wanted to sell, she would be in a better place to do so. He had gotten so excited talking about the work he could do, it had been impossible not to get her hopes up.

He'd played on her desire to succeed and she knew that, but she let him. What could it hurt? He wasn't asking for money and agreed he'd let her know what supplies he needed and she'd buy them. No more digging in dumpsters for dented cans or asking his uncle for donations. If she wasn't paying for labor, she could afford the supplies.

And if it gave someone else who was down on his luck a break, why shouldn't she take advantage of his offer?

"I think I'm going to hold off on selling the café," she said.

Marcus lifted his brows. "Oh. What changed your mind?"

She leaned on the table and looked around. "I'm just not ready to give up yet."

He hid it well, but she saw the flash of disappointment before he forced a reassuring smile. "Then you shouldn't give up yet, Jen."

"I know what you're thinking—"

"That I'm happy for you."

"That you're sick and tired of fixing pipes and toilets and sinks and everything else. I hear you, Marcus. I agree. I am, too. But I found a handyman, and I want to try to salvage this place."

He lifted his brows with immediate curiosity. "Who?"

"His name is Daniel. He needs some side projects while he

gets on his feet and can do just about everything I need. He looked over my wish list and is taking on what fits in my budget."

The same surprise he'd had when he noticed the fresh paint returned. "Oh. Good. How were his references?"

She stared at him.

"Don't tell me you hired this guy without references."

"Marcus—"

"You got references, didn't you?"

She frowned at him. "I am perfectly capable of hiring a handyman."

"But how do you know he's qualified?"

She gestured to the wall. "He managed to paint, didn't he?"

"That's a million miles away from the things that need to be done to this place."

"Marcus. Stop. Please. You have your hands full running your business. Let me run mine."

He pressed his lips together. "I'm not trying to run your business. I'm just looking out for my sister."

"I know that. But if this guy turns out to be worthless, I'm not out anything."

"Except however much you're paying him. How much are you paying him?"

Instead of answering, she leaned back. "I know it's hard to believe, but I'm not completely incompetent."

"I didn't—"

"I know you didn't say it. But we've both thought it over the last three years." She shrugged. "I've relied on you too much. Before I throw in the towel, I'd like to try it on my own. This guy needs the work, and I need the help."

"I would have liked to have met him. Asked him a few questions."

"I asked him plenty of questions. He's qualified to do what I need and can work within my budget. That is all I need to know." She looked out the window and her heart lifted. "Look who's here."

Seconds later the door opened and Marcus's stepdaughter walked in with her own soon-to-be-stepdaughter pushing by her.

"Marcus!" Jessica beamed, making a beeline for the table Jenna was sharing with her brother.

She watched as Marcus enveloped the girl. Jess was going on twelve now, but her Down syndrome made it difficult to know her age by looking at her. In some ways, she was wise beyond her years. In others, she was still a little girl. But all of her was completely lovable.

"Hi, Jen," Jess said before giving Jenna her own big hug.

She smiled when the girl leaned back and grinned up at her. Every time Jenna saw that smile, she swore she fell in love with her a little more. "I'm guessing you want liver and onions for lunch."

She scrunched her nose. "Ew!"

"Just liver?"

"*Jenna*! You know what I want!"

"Oh, you want a Jessica Special." Which translated to rainbow pancakes with whipped topping, a side of bacon, and orange juice.

"Of course!"

Jenna gave her one more kiss on the head and then exchanged a quick hug with Mallory. "Hey, kiddo. Your mom coming, too?"

"No. She's having lunch with Kara today. Pretty sure they are not so subtly planning some kind of engagement party for me and Phil."

"With superheroes," Jess said seriously. "It's not a party without superheroes."

"No, it isn't," Mallory agreed, scooting in next to Jess. "I'll have what she's having."

"With coffee," Jenna said before Mal could.

"And you?" she asked her brother.

"Burger and fries."

"Mom will kill you if she sees you eating that," Mallory warned.

"Your cholesterol is too high," Jess reminded him.

"Chicken sandwich, grilled," he corrected. "Applesauce instead of fries."

Jenna smiled as she walked away while Marcus asked Mallory if he should be planning some kind of party with her fiancé's father. Jenna was so happy for her brother—he finally had the family he'd always wanted, even if it were a few decades later than planned and the girl he now considered his daughter was old enough to be married. Jenna envied him, if she were being honest. Even with all the ups and downs and challenges of helping Annie recover from her injury and his diet-altering high cholesterol, Marcus had a life worth envying.

She'd hoped for that kind of life with Peter, but she'd ended up living more like a butterfly pinned to a cushion in a display case. Pretty to look at, but without much purpose. His career didn't have room for all the mess of having children and he needed Jenna focused on the details of helping him succeed. How could she possibly raise a family when she was too busy polishing Peter's culinary star?

She'd come to terms with not having kids soon after her divorce. And now she had Mallory, and Jess, and Phil—Mallory's soon-to-be-husband. And Jenna imagined they'd have a family. Not to mention all the people that came through the café on a regular basis. Her life and her heart were full. Even so, she wouldn't have minded having what Marcus and Annie had. The kind of rock-solid unconditional love they'd found wasn't something Jenna ever expected to come her way, but she wouldn't have minded having it.

No. She wouldn't have minded having that at all.

Daniel stepped into the kitchen as Jenna was chopping carrots for the next day's special. "Pick one."

She looked at the binder he held open. The images were of

two different styles of booth covers. One solid red, the other blue-and-white striped. Both were images she'd tucked into her plan book for the café, but he couldn't do both.

He tapped the picture with the red vinyl. "This will be cheaper. Significantly."

She wiped her hands on a towel as she met his gaze. "Then go with that."

The hesitancy in her voice gave him pause. "If you want the blue—"

"It's not that."

He lowered the book. "What is it?"

She bit her lip and glanced away before looking in his eyes again. "Can you really do all the things you say?"

"By that I assume you mean reupholster your booths?"

"And the plumbing and the electrical and everything else you were talking about at breakfast."

"Yes. I'll know more about the plumbing and electrical once I dig into that, but I suspect as old as this building is, you'll need all new pipes and a full rewire. My uncle can help if needed. I want to work out the budget first."

"Are you licensed to do those things in Iowa?"

"Yes. I told you, I worked construction."

"How much do you charge per hour?"

He shook his head. "I don't want—"

"Look, it's great that you replaced my window locks for turkey and mashed potatoes, but that won't cover your time, Daniel."

"I'm perfectly happy with turkey and mashed potatoes." He grinned, thinking about the food that had filled his stomach before he went to work on cleaning up the dining room for her. "And an occasional meatloaf dinner."

"You said to give you one month, right?"

"Yeah. I can't get everything done, but I can get a good start."

She took the binder from him. Dropping her collection of dreams on the counter with a thud, she crossed her arms over her chest again. She was clearly debating something. "Follow me."

"Okay," he muttered as she snagged her keys and headed for the kitchen door.

She walked up the stairs she took every night, bypassing the platform that led to her apartment, and kept climbing to the third floor. She unlocked the door and flipped a light switch on as she stepped inside. "One of the many things on my to-do list is turning this space into a rental. I wanted to finish the café first. No need to tell you how that's been going. It's a bit of a mess and there's no furniture, but it's a roof, electricity, and running water. So that's a step up, right?"

"Jenna—"

She met his gaze. "I'm not comfortable taking handouts any more than you are. You know as well as I do even if you eat three meals a day at the café, that is not going to offset what I should be paying you for your time. This"—she gestured around at the dusty space—"isn't much, but it's better than sleeping behind a dumpster in an alley, and it makes me feel that we're at least close to even."

He stepped deeper into the loft apartment. The space had likely been used for storage years ago. The open concept made the apartment feel huge, but if he actually had furniture to put in the room, it would fill quickly. A line of cabinets, some with doors hanging on by broken hinges, lined one wall. Below that was a dingy yellow counter and sink. A fridge sat on the same wall as the only door in the space—one he suspected would lead to the bathroom. Large-paned windows rarely seen in today's architecture adorned the rest of the walls. The space would be beautiful if cleaned and repaired properly.

No. It wasn't much at the moment, but as she had said, it was definitely a step up from the alley.

Swallowing, he met her gaze. "I can fix this space up, too. Make it ready to rent when you're ready."

"Let's update the café first. If there's anything left in my budget, we'll talk about what can be done here. I cleaned up a little bit, but didn't have time to scrub the floors. You can bring up cleaning supplies from the café. Just be sure to return them when you're done. And I didn't know what kind of toiletries you used, but there are some things in the bathroom. There's some food in what passes as the kitchen. Sorry I couldn't do anything about the lack of a bed, but I'll ask around. Maybe someone has one they'll sell for cheap."

"No. Don't…" He met her gaze and smiled. "Don't put yourself out. I've got my bag."

She slipped a key off the ring in her hand and held it out to him. He tightened his fist around the small bit of metal. He had a key. To a door. That was his for at least a month. A quiet laugh left him.

"Thank you, Jenna. I promise I'm going to make your café amazing."

Her lip twitched with a grin. "I hope you keep your promises better than most men."

CHAPTER SIX

*J*enna sat up in bed, her breath stuck in her throat. She didn't know what had woken her until blue light flickered behind her curtain. She exhaled slowly as thunder thudded across the sky like a bowling ball rolling over an uneven floor. Wind whistled for a moment, the pitch accentuated in the tunnel created by the building next to hers, and then the rain started peck-peck-pecking against her window.

A quick glance at the clock told her it was nearly four a.m. She pulled the blankets around her shoulders, silently counting when her window brightened again. *One-two-three...*

Rumble.

Then another sound caught her attention. Something heavy had been tossed down. In the bed of a truck. Her stomach dropped. She'd hesitantly left the café unlocked when she'd finally called it a night. Daniel had wanted to pull off some of the old paneling so he could check the condition of the walls before they went to Carson's Hardware to get the supplies he needed to put up new wainscoting. Obviously he couldn't do that when the café was open, and she couldn't stay up all night supervising. She had wavered between trusting her gut where Daniel was concerned, hearing Marcus warn her against hiring someone without the proper references and remembering Peter mocking her for being too trusting.

She'd gone with her instinct and trusted Daniel to be in her café without her—and to have a key to lock up when he was done. And now someone was tossing heavy items into the bed of a truck just outside her window.

Had he left the café open? Was someone stripping the kitchen of all her expensive equipment to sell for profit?

Was *he* stripping her kitchen?

Jumping out of bed, Jenna flipped the locks on her front door —Marcus had installed three—and rushed down the stairs, squinting at the truck in an attempt to commit the make and model to memory so she could file a proper police report. The truck was black. Maybe dark blue. Big. Dual tires in the back. There was something written on the tailgate.

Burke Construction, along with a phone number.

Burke Construction?

Daniel had said his uncle owned a construction company. And that he was borrowing a truck.

She looked to the café's kitchen door when a man stepped out carrying a sheet of paneling. He tossed it in the back and the sound echoed through the alley. Guilt and a bit of shame washed over Jenna. As much as she'd wanted to trust Daniel, she hadn't. She hadn't trusted him not to steal. Not to leave her door open. To take care of the things he'd said he'd take care of.

He turned and jerked to a stop when he locked eyes on her.

The rain had increased and his hair and T-shirt started clinging to his skin as he stood there. Finally, he took a few steps. "Jenna, are you okay?"

No. She wasn't okay. She was mortified by the depth of her doubt in him. He'd proven himself reliable more than once, and she still didn't believe him. But trust hadn't come easily to her for a long time. So many people in her past had taken her confidence in them and used it against her. She closed her eyes to stop her train of thought before looking at Daniel again.

Though his broad chest and brooding look would frighten most who crossed him in a dark side street at four in the morning, she only felt shame. "Y-Yes. I'm...fine. I heard a noise. I thought there might be trouble."

He flicked his gaze over her before staring into her eyes. "So you came running out like that to investigate?"

Startled, she glanced down at herself. A thin charcoal-colored tank top and tiny shorts were all that protected her from being naked. She wasn't wearing a bra, but thankfully the dim light made it difficult to see the effect the cool night air was having on her. Even so, she crossed her arms over her breasts.

Something flashed in his eyes when she looked at him again.

She couldn't quite determine was it was, but his voice was clipped when he spoke again.

"Get back inside, Jenna."

She glanced at the truck. He followed her gaze.

"My uncle has a dumpster on his work site. I can toss this there instead of you paying to have it hauled away. Unless you want to pay to have it hauled away."

She shook her head and rain-damp strands clung to her cheeks. "No."

He stared her down, and she knew he'd seen through her excuse before he said the words.

"You thought I was stealing."

Guilt hit her again. "No. I...I thought you forgot to lock up and someone else was stealing."

She hadn't had to say what her next thought had been. She had considered the possibility that he was robbing her blind. Though the light in the alley was hazy, she saw the change in his eyes as he clearly heard what she hadn't said. She'd hurt him by not trusting him. She wanted to explain. She had a way of trusting the wrong people. She was a terrible judge of character and had been burned before. But the words stuck in her throat.

"Go inside," he said more gently before turning away from her. "I've got to get this mess cleaned up and the truck back to my uncle's site."

"I can help—"

He walked away and she exhaled a harsh breath before heading back up the stairs. Once inside her apartment, she looked at the bed, but knew she'd never get back to sleep. What was the point anyway? She'd have to be up in an hour to start getting ready for work.

She rushed through the shower to get the chill of the rain off her skin and then tossed on her usual café attire—jeans and an old T-shirt—before pulling her hair up in a bun and heading downstairs to offer the best apology she could muster to the man going out of his way to help her.

Daniel did his best to push the image of Jenna standing half-naked from his mind. She'd come flying down the stairs to what —catch him stealing? Stop him from stealing? What if she'd been right? What if there had been trouble in the alley?

What the hell was she going to do? Did she even know basic self-defense?

And wearing...*that*. Two flimsy bits of material that barely covered her.

Jesus. She was going to get herself hurt. She had no idea how dangerous the world could be.

No wonder he felt compelled to look after her. Raking his hand over his hair, pushing the too-long strands from his eyes, he went back into the café to gather the rest of the paneling he'd pulled off the walls. He was pushing the broom across the dining room floor when he heard her light footsteps enter from the kitchen.

"The walls look a little rough right now, but if you can find time to go to the hardware store with me today, we should be able to get everything I need to get the new wainscoting up tonight after you close. When I stopped in, they said they can deliver the board same day as long as they have it in stock."

"Daniel," she said softly, "I'm sorry."

He shook his head at her apology. "Don't be." He pushed the broom a bit harder than necessary. "You should be on guard. You don't know me."

"I hurt your feelings. That wasn't my intent."

He finally stopped to look at her. Thankfully, she'd gotten dressed. Jeans and her usual vintage T-shirt. This one of the Moody Blues. He smiled slightly. "I like '70s music, too. Reminds me of my mom."

She creased her brow. "What?"

"All your shirts are of '70s musicians."

She looked down at herself, much like she'd done in the alley…and the night he'd rushed into the kitchen and pointed out that she was soaking wet. This time, when she met his eyes again, she wasn't horrified. She was clearly confused. "Uh, I guess. I never really thought about it much." She offered him a weak smile. "Daniel, I'm sorry I doubted you. You've been very kind to me—"

"You'd have to be gullible to trust me completely." His suggestion caused her back to stiffen and her eyes to narrow a bit. He'd struck a nerve.

"I'm not gullible."

He took a few seconds to digest her response. Something about his accusation angered her. Maybe because Marcus seemed to be so overprotective. Jenna probably resented that, but Daniel understood where her brother was coming from. She had an air of innocence about her that made Daniel want to protect her, too.

She took a step closer. "Let me clean this up. It's the least I can do after you were up all night working."

"I don't mind. I'll sleep when I'm done."

"Please. Let me sweep this up. You take your uncle's truck to him. I'll have breakfast ready when you get back so you can get some rest. Unless you want me to follow you in my car and give you a ride back."

"No. It's not far." He handed over the broom and left without another word, locking the kitchen door behind him as he went.

He pulled out of the alley and headed to Charlie's construction site a mile or so away. The rain had eased but was still falling steadily. Jenna's doubt in him stung, but he hadn't lied to her when he pointed out that she was right to be on guard around him. She didn't know him, yet she'd not only given him access to her business, but had given him a place to live above her. She was too nice for her own good. If he had the wrong intentions toward her, she had given him all the opportunity he'd need to harm her.

Sighing, he tightened his hands on the steering wheel at the idea of someone taking advantage of her kindness—or, worse, hurting her. He wouldn't be living in her building forever. He had to move on eventually and the next person she rented to might not be as honorable. He decided that he'd give her at least the most basic skills she'd need to handle a bad situation.

Lesson one: don't go running out into a dark alley in the middle of the night scantily clad to face perceived danger.

Shaking his head, he again had to force the image of her in a tank top and short-shorts from his mind. Her big brown eyes seemed so sad when she'd looked at him. Like her mistrust had hurt her more than him.

Speaking of lack of trust... A witless laugh left Daniel when he noticed his uncle parked next to the small trailer that held his mobile office. In the weeks that he'd worked with Charlie, they hadn't arrived onsite any earlier than seven. It wasn't even five thirty yet.

Someone else who didn't trust him.

He'd been honest when he told Jenna she'd be crazy to trust a homeless man she'd just met—even if seeing the doubt in her eyes had cut at his pride in a way that was unexpected—but seeing his uncle here, waiting for his equipment to be returned, stung Daniel. He'd never conned his uncle. That was his dad, and he was damned tired of Charlie seeing him in the same light.

Sure, he'd screwed up plenty in his life, but he'd never deceived or stolen from anyone.

He drove past the office to the dumpster. He was lifting the third panel out of the truck when Charlie approached. "I told you I'd have everything back on time. You didn't need to check on me."

"I wasn't checking on you," he said, grabbing an end of the panel to help lift it over the side of the dumpster.

Daniel rested his arm on the truck bed and looked at his uncle with disbelief. "You just happened to be here at five in the morning?"

Charlie stared at him for a minute before smirking. "You never told me where you were taking my truck and equipment."

Grabbing the last panel, Daniel went back to emptying the truck bed. "Stonehill Café."

"Oh, I know the place. You're fixing it up, huh?"

He wasn't really in the mood for conversation after the two most important people in his life had looked at him with suspicion in a span of less than an hour. Grunting as he tossed the last panel in, he took a breath and wondered what the hell it said about him that the two most important people in his life were a woman he barely knew and a man who seemed to only tolerate him because of his dead mother.

Putting his hands on his hips, he faced Charlie. "The owner gave me a place to crash and a few meals a day to fix her place up. It's something to do while I get my head worked out."

Charlie nodded slowly as he digested this information. "She's a nice woman from what I've heard."

"She's a very nice woman. Don't worry. I'm not going to do anything to screw her over."

"I didn't say—"

"You didn't have to." He started around his uncle. "Keys are in the ignition. Tools are in the box. Everything is clean and where it goes."

"Hey, wait." Charlie caught up to him. "Danny. I am worried about you. I promised—"

"Mom that you'd take care of me," Daniel finished. "I'm a grown man now, Charlie. Even if Mom were here, she couldn't take any better care of me than you have. You've done your job."

"Would you just… Come here."

Daniel followed him into the office. Charlie gestured to his duffel bag in the corner. He'd squeezed what he could in his backpack when he'd left, but it hadn't been much. The rest had been left in the guest room closet with a promise to pick it up as soon as he could. Seeing the bag pricked at his heart. Charlie couldn't get rid of him fast enough, apparently.

"You said yesterday that you had a place to stay, so I thought you should have your things, too. If your situation changes, you can always bring them back. I'm happy to hang on to them for you, but I thought you might want a change of clothes. And maybe a shave."

Daniel instinctively ran his hand over his unkempt beard. He couldn't remember the last time he'd looked so out of sorts. He nodded and tossed the bag over his shoulder. "Thanks."

"Let me give you a ride."

Daniel was bone-tired after an evening of replacing window locks and a night of tearing out paneling and sanding the walls to make them somewhat aesthetically pleasing for Jenna's customers. The walk back to the café suddenly seemed daunting.

He gave his uncle a curt nod and dropped his bag in the back of the truck before climbing into the passenger side.

"What kind of work are you doing over there?" Charlie asked.

"Right now, I'm just doing some cosmetics to the dining room. She hasn't been able to do much to update since buying the place three years ago. It's pretty run-down. I painted and did some minor repairs on tables to get them through until she can put more into it. I pulled the old paneling last night. We're going to go get some wainscoting today if she has time. That'll go up tonight."

"So, uh… You're working at night."

"Yeah. Can't really sand the walls when people are eating."

"No. No. You can't do that around her customers."

The tone in Charlie's voice said more than his words. Daniel deserved his uncle's uncertainty. His temper had put Charlie in not one but two awkward situations. The first with his crew, and the other with his wife. He'd tried to justify to both that Daniel had just left the army and needed time to adjust. That was the excuse Daniel had used, after all. Even so, he hated that the only person he could call family was so distrusting.

"I'm not around her customers. I'm not even around her much. She's safe."

"I know *she* is," he said quietly. "I just worry about anyone who might get disgruntled over bad service or a bill or…anybody who looks at her in a way you don't like."

Daniel inhaled. Yup. He had earned this. "She knows about

my history. I let her know that I have issues before I started working for her." He looked up at the café when Charlie parked at the curb. Jenna wasn't in the dining room, but knowing she was in the building brought a strange sense of serenity. "Remember how Mom always wanted to take care of everyone?"

"Yeah," Charlie said quietly. "She was a good person. Had a good heart. That's why she gave your dad so many chances to redeem himself."

Daniel ignored the jab at his father. "Jenna reminds me of Mom. She's kind and patient. Too trusting, but not stupid. She doesn't trust me yet. But she's trying to. I'm not going to make her regret that." He glanced at his uncle. "Maybe someday, after I get my head together, you'll be ready to give me another chance. If you do, I won't make you regret it either."

He hopped out before his uncle could respond. Grabbing his bag from the truck bed, he walked through the alley and into the café. Jenna had promised him breakfast. He didn't want to keep her waiting.

CHAPTER SEVEN

*J*enna had barely finished pouring syrup on her pancakes when the heavy silence between Daniel and her became too much. Guilt found her again. She bit her lips as she set the bottle down. "I was a culinary student when I met my ex-husband. I'd gotten into this fancy school just outside of San Francisco. I was so proud. It was the first step to so many things I wanted to accomplish. One day this guest chef comes in, and I was immediately smitten. He was the most handsome man I'd ever seen and he seemed to be genuinely interested in me. He said I had this Midwestern charm that was quite the novelty for a city boy like him."

She stared at her food, but nothing on her plate looked appetizing. "Before I knew it, we were inseparable and he was making all these big promises about how successful we were going to be. *We*. Always *we*. *We* were going to open restaurants. *We* were going to be the next hot spot. But in order for that to happen, he needed me to give him one hundred percent. He convinced me to drop out of school—which Marcus threatened to kill me over—and I focused everything I had on Peter's plan. Then we got engaged and... Well, that's when I should have figured out he was swindling me. As if convincing me to drop out of the institute wasn't enough, before long he was convincing me to invest my inheritance in his plan. A little here and there, and just to help us...always *us*...get noticed. Then he started systematically breaking me down. You know how some people have a way of cutting you and then convincing you that you aren't bleeding? That was Peter. He'd smile while he was ripping my heart out and tell me it was for my own good. And I believed him."

She cast a glance Daniel's way to see if he was listening. The intensity in his eyes caused heat to touch her cheeks. Embarrassment at the story she was telling. "He said before he'd marry me, I had to drop twenty pounds because while he didn't mind a little extra weight, he didn't want people commenting negatively on my appearance and hurting my feelings. So I did. I lost weight, he married me, and I kept investing until everything my parents had left me was gone. By then success started rolling in. But it was no longer we. It was him. All him. We were no longer a team. I was barely his wife. He didn't have time for me anymore. He was too busy being Peter Reid—Sweetheart of the San Fran Dining Scene. Every dream I had, every plan for my future was...nothing to him. *I* was nothing to him. One night, I reached my limit. I hadn't seen him for more than an hour or two at a time for weeks. He was always traveling, always doing interviews, and catering parties for the elite. I packed a bag, more in a pathetic attempt to get him to notice me than anything else, and headed for my best friend's house. I'd tried to call her to let her know I was coming, but she didn't answer."

Jenna swallowed as she felt tears bite at the backs of her eyes. She hadn't thought about that moment for so long, she was surprised it still had the power to break her. "She also didn't answer her door when I knocked, but I knew where she kept her key. I walked in and there they were. Sitting in fancy bathrobes cuddling in front of a fire, looking like quite the happy couple. I can't recall how many times I'd told her what he meant to me and how much he was hurting me, and she always said he didn't deserve me. She had been trying to convince me to leave him for months. I thought she was trying to protect me. She just wanted him for herself. I trusted them. I trusted both of them and they just..."

She drew a breath as she looked down. Her breakfast blurred as the tears moved from the back of her eyes to the front. She blinked and sniffed and sighed before looking at him. "He, um, he'd told me that we couldn't have kids because he was so busy. They have two now. Last I heard anyway. They moved to L.A. and success continues to roll in. That's okay. Look what I have," she said lightly as she gestured around the café.

She dropped her hands and finally dared to look at Daniel. He was staring, his eyes hard and, if she had to guess, angry. "I'd been stupid enough to sign a prenuptial agreement. Again, he'd said that was for my own good. I was the one with assets when we got married, but I gave up everything to help him. I literally walked away with a suitcase of clothes because I hadn't *officially* worked a single day of our marriage. While I'd done all the grunt work of building his career, I was never paid. My time was never put in the books. On paper, I looked like the moocher and I was treated as such in the divorce. I was foolish and blind and I trusted the wrong people, Daniel. I gave away everything I had and got nothing in return. It's not you, okay? It's me. I don't trust myself to make the right decisions or to believe in the right people. You haven't done anything to warrant my mistrust. I just don't have much faith in myself. I'm sorry I let my issues hurt you."

She swallowed when he continued to stare at her. "I just poured my heart out to you. Could you say something?"

Finally he broke the intense eye contact and cut into his stack of pancakes. "I'm going to teach you self-defense."

She tilted her head and creased her brow. "Huh?"

"Just some basic moves in case you ever need them."

She opened her mouth and then closed it again. "What does that have to do with my trust issues?"

"You're sitting in an empty café with a man who has been trained to kill with his bare hands and who also has admitted to having a temper bad enough to get him discharged from the US Army. You don't have nearly as many trust issues as you think, Jenna."

Laughter bubbled up in her chest and escaped before she

could stop it. "Wow. I hadn't thought of all that. Good point. Very good point. So maybe stupidity is my issue?"

"Considering what my life is like right now, I don't think you even have issues."

Picking up her fork, she poked at her egg until the yolk broke. Though her food was cold now, she dipped her bacon in the goo and took a healthy bite. "Why do you want to teach me self-defense? If you bring up the colander incident, I'm spitting in your lunch."

"Because you can't defend yourself with a strainer." He grinned. "Your threat is idle to a man who eats out of a dumpster."

She leaned back as she giggled. "Okay, listen, if you're going to counter everything I say with this sarcastic brand of logic you've developed, we'll no longer be talking over breakfast."

He nodded as he chewed the last of his pancakes and then washed them down with coffee. "How about this?" As he leaned over the table, his eyes lost all their merriment and his usual intensity returned. "I've been living in your alley for weeks and you had no idea you were being watched. I broke into your building twice. You have a tendency to leave the kitchen door unlocked, usually wide open, while you are cleaning up after a long day of taking *cash* payments. Your routine never alters. You walk up a dimly lit flight of stairs in the dark every single night. You live alone. You're a beautiful woman. You're *too* trusting of strangers. When faced with the danger of a man looming over you in your kitchen, your first instinct was to recoil. The first time you thought someone was robbing your café you ran down dark stairs into an alley without any kind of weapon and wearing clothes that could have been torn from your body in a matter of seconds. If I had any malicious intent toward you, Jenna, you could have been raped, robbed, and murdered countless times over the last few weeks. And what would you have done to stop me?"

She swallowed hard as all the images played out in her mind. However, none of the villains in her mind were Daniel. She might not have known him well, but she knew in her heart that he'd never hurt her. But he was right. That didn't mean someone else wouldn't.

"When do we start?"

"We'll train tonight after you close."

She lifted her brows. "*Train?*"

"Two hours a day."

"Two hours?"

"Minimum."

"Every day?"

He stared at her, dead serious, but finally, he cracked a smile and she exhaled with relief.

She tossed her napkin at him. "I liked you better when you were hiding behind the dumpster."

His smile widened and he laughed, and Jenna couldn't help but join him.

sh

Daniel woke with a start. He glanced around the room, needing a few seconds to orient himself. Finally he recognized Jenna's empty apartment. Letting out a breath, he closed his eyes and tried to push the images that had haunted him while he slept. For years he'd relived moments from his childhood—his drunk father throwing punches, his mother crying as she begged for mercy while Daniel peeked out from the crack in the closet door, wishing he was brave enough to protect her.

Only this dream wasn't about his parents.

Jenna had been screaming and Daniel couldn't reach her. He had been stuck behind the dumpster while she begged him to help her. He had pushed against the bin with all his strength, but it wouldn't budge. He had screamed her name to let her know he was there, he was trying, but some unseen force was keeping him away from her. Finally, the screaming stopped and he was able to run into the café.

There she was, soaking wet in her jeans and Barry Manilow T-shirt, lying on the floor with a fucking strainer in her hand. He scooped her up, but it was too late. Her beautiful brown eyes were wide open and lifeless.

"I told you this would happen," Charlie had said from the swinging doors. "You're just like your dad, kid."

Now, as Daniel lay there catching his breath, he realized he was the one that was soaked. Sweat had beaded on his forehead and when he dragged his hand over his face his hair clung to him.

"Son of a bitch," he whispered as he pushed the sleeping bag open and headed right to the bathroom. He splashed water on his face before taking a look at his reflection. He'd stopped shaving when he'd gotten back to the States. The freedom to grow his hair long had been too tempting to ignore. Now he looked like what he was—a bum.

Digging in the shaving kit that had been returned to him in his duffel bag, Daniel found his electric razor. Pushing the button, he tested the battery, happy to find it still active. He put a guard on the blade and went to work on cleaning the scruffy hair from his face. He focused on his task to stop the memory of how Jenna's eyes had grown terrified as he ran down all the ways he could have hurt her from flashing through his mind. He'd intentionally scared her. He wanted her to know how serious the situation was. She was vulnerable, and she needed to know it.

He'd noticed the three locks on her door, which was good. But he'd also noticed the window next to her front door had the same flimsy lock as the one he'd so easily jimmied to get into her café. He needed to replace that as well. He was also going to talk to her about a security system. He understood the expense was a concern, but not nearly as much of a concern as her safety.

Stonehill wasn't immune to crime, though everyone here seemed to live as if it were. Even Charlie and Lisa would often go to bed without checking the locks on the door. Daniel was convinced one of the things that made Lisa so uneasy was that he had pointed out that they were practically asking to be robbed. His assessment had probably planted the seed that he was intending to pawn all their goods.

He hoped he didn't plant the seed in Jenna's mind that he was planning to harm her. He'd never touch her like that. But she needed to understand that she was putting herself at risk. Then she needed to know how to hurt someone enough to get away from immediate danger.

Brushing the cut hairs from his face, Daniel looked at the wayward hair on his head. Grabbing handful after handful, he gave himself a much-needed cut. By the time he was done, he could see his old self again. He was more reminiscent of stone-hard and determined Colonel Maguire than the bumbling civilian failing to rebuild his life. He wasn't quite back to looking like his old self. He'd lost weight. He'd aged. His eyes looked hollow. And haunted.

Turning his attention away from the ghost in his reflection, he focused on cleaning out the sink and then stood under the shower head, letting the hot water ease some of the tension in his shoulders. While he'd love to stand there for hours, he was more than aware of the fact that Jenna was the one paying the utilities. He dried off with the towel she had provided for him, brushed his teeth, and dressed in clothes he hadn't worn in weeks. While he didn't mind trading the same couple outfits, it was nice to put on something different.

Opening the windows, he let fresh air into the apartment and looked around the kitchen, debating where to start. He'd brought up a few essentials from the shelf where Jenna kept her tools, so he decided the first thing was getting the cabinet doors reattached. Once those were up, he pulled out some of the rags he'd also brought from the café and started wiping the surfaces down. By the time he was done, his stomach was growling. He'd already gotten spoiled by Jenna's willingness to feed him. A quick glance at his watch confirmed it was just past the café's lunchtime, or what would become his breakfast, since he would be working overnight and sleeping the morning away.

After washing his hands, he gathered the tools and dirty towels and headed down to the café. He walked into the kitchen without knocking...he didn't have to; the damned door was open.

Jenna glanced toward him and then paused and blinked several times before standing upright. "You're...bald."

Running a hand over his head, he chuckled. "Not quite bald, but close enough. This is much better."

"Agreed."

He touched his chin next. "It was nice to see my face."

"It's a nice face to be seen." She snapped her mouth shut and a flood of red tinted her cheeks. "I just mean...it's nice to see you cleaned up. Um. Scott?"

The kid at the grill turned, and Daniel's dislike for him didn't ease up. He had earbuds in and looked annoyed that his boss dared to interrupt him. "Yeah?"

"This is Daniel. He's doing some work for me around here. You'll see him coming in and out. He eats for free."

His response was a nod before returning to his task. Daniel let his breath out slowly. The little shit should have shown more respect to his boss, but as Charlie had reminded Daniel a hundred times, he'd save himself a lot of trouble by minding his own business.

"Speaking of eating," Jenna said in her usual happy tone. "Hungry?"

"Yeah. Actually, I am. I thought we could head over to the hardware store if you have time. I don't want to wait too late or they may not deliver today. I'd like to get the wainscoting up tonight."

"That'd be great. What do you want to eat?"

"Whatever you feed me."

By the time he'd put the tools on the shelf and come back, she was covering a mound of real mashed potatoes with chicken and noodles—the day's special. *Yes!*

She added a smaller portion of the same to another plate and backed out of the kitchen as Daniel followed. She eased their plates onto a table where there was a tub with utensils waiting to be rolled up in napkins. After setting that aside, she slid into the booth and dug into her lunch. "I was thinking about what you said this morning."

"Which part?"

She glanced up at him and chuckled. "I'm sorry. You're going to have to give me a day or two to get used to the new you."

He instinctively stroked his chin again. "This is actually the old me. On the surface anyway."

She returned her focus to her food. "You're right about how unprepared I am to defend myself. You've heard me say that my sister-in-law is disabled, but she hasn't always been. She was shot during an attempted robbery, and she'll never fully recover. I know," she quickly added, "nothing you can teach me will stop a bullet, but I can't keep pretending like nothing bad could ever happen to me. All the things you pointed out put me at high risk. I should at least have an idea what to do."

He nodded. "I'm glad you see it that way. I was actually afraid I'd gone too far. I don't want you to be afraid of me. I would never do those things." Grunts had used to give him the same wide-eyed, terrified stare that he had gotten from Jenna. Seeing that look on kids just coming into boot camp had given him never-ending amusement. Watching Jenna's face melt into horror hadn't been nearly as fun.

"I know. I get what you were saying and you were right. You may be a good guy. But maybe the next man who finds his way to my alley won't be. I have to prepare for that."

"Yes, you do."

"You know, I spent ten years living in San Francisco, but I was in a bubble. I guess that's part of the Midwestern charm Peter always pointed out. A nice way to say naïve. Which is a nicer way to say ignorant."

Daniel drew a breath and exhaled slowly so that when he spoke, he didn't sound as frustrated as he felt. "You've said that more than once, and I've let it slide, but now I'm setting you straight."

She lifted her brows at him, but he didn't stop despite the surprise on her face.

"You got taken advantage of by someone you trusted. That

doesn't make you stupid, Jenna. It makes you human. What you have to do now is shake it off and move on. You're doing better at that than you give yourself credit for."

"Oh, please. Look at this place. It's a disaster."

"*You* look at this place." He used his fork to point toward the four elderly women sitting in a corner booth. They were always laughing and their conversation never seemed to lull. "I see them here several times a week. What's their story?"

"They're all widows. They have coffee every other morning. Usually talking about grandkids and planning church events. It's more about the companionship, but I don't think any of them would admit that. They need to feel that their little group is working toward something, even if it is just a potluck dinner in the church basement."

"And that guy?" he asked of the man who came in at least twice a week and sat at the counter. He always seemed too busy scribbling in a notebook to talk to anyone, but Daniel had noticed how he'd pause and smile at Jenna and Sara when they refilled his coffee mug.

"He's a writer who just needs that one big break," she said with a smile.

"And this guy?" He pointed to himself.

Her smile softened. "A guy who's a little down on his luck and needs someone to give him a chance."

He nodded. "And you?"

"A hot mess trying to pull herself together."

"You know the building might be a little run-down right

now, but you're working on fixing it up. Kind of how every single person here is working on fixing themselves in some way. We'd all be the same people going through the same problems without the café, Jenna, but isn't it nice how we all seem to have found a place here?"

She met his gaze again, and there was a sheen in her eyes. Shit. He hadn't meant to make her cry. He'd only wanted her to think about how the café was more than just a building. He was about to apologize when she sat a bit taller and smiled.

"I hadn't thought of it like that. I only see the cracks and dings. But you're right. It's a work in progress. Just like all the people sitting here." She sighed and nodded as if processing his words. "You know, I always feel guilty when I need Marcus to come help me with something, and he always says it gives him a chance to work on something he can actually fix. I guess I never considered what he meant by that. Can you imagine watching someone you love hurting and not being able to help her? He has to feel pretty powerless sometimes."

Daniel gave his head a quick shake as images from his childhood tried to enter his mind. "It's not an easy thing to go through. He probably needs this café as much as you do. I know it's overwhelming sometimes, but so is life. If you give up on the café, you'll just have a different kind of hurdle to overcome."

She put her hand on his and squeezed. "Thank you, Daniel. I've been feeling really sorry for myself lately. Walking away from the café seemed like the only answer, but giving up on my dream isn't going to make me feel better. In fact, it will make things much worse." She nodded. "Time to let go of past mistakes and move on, right?"

"Exactly."

"For both of us."

The smirk on her face wasn't lost on him, nor was the fact that her hand was still on his. He tightened his fingers around hers, taking a moment to soak up her touch. He would have liked to hold on to her kindness forever, but that wasn't an option. He pulled his hand back and nodded. "Finish your lunch, and we'll see what we can do about replacing this paneling."

CHAPTER EIGHT

*J*enna's breath caught when Daniel gripped her wrist and pulled her to him.

He held her gaze for what seemed like a lifetime. His dark eyes stared into hers, and his breath whispered across her face like feathers. She swallowed hard, debating what she should do. Before she could decide her next move, he frowned and released his hold on her.

"Jenna."

She shrugged as her cheeks warmed. "I'm sorry. I just don't want to hurt you."

"Yes, you do," he countered. "If I grab you with the intention of hurting you, you most certainly do want to hurt me."

"No, I mean…"

"I know what you mean, but you don't want to wait until you're being attacked to figure out how to use what I'm teaching you. Now, come on. Break away from me."

She braced herself. "Okay."

This time when he yanked her, she stepped into his move and turned.

"Raise your elbow as you spin," he reminded her. "Now slam your arm down."

She did, but he didn't release her.

"Harder, Jenna. You aren't going to get away like that." Releasing her, he let her step back. "Stop worrying about hurting me. I'm teaching you how to hurt me. Do it again."

They repeated the move, but when she failed to break his hold this time, he startled her by roughly yanking her back against his chest. He wrapped his fingers around her jaw as his other arm pinned her against him. His hold on her was firm but gentle. Still, she felt a sense of panic, mostly because he'd been able to pin her without much effort.

He put his lips close to her ear. "Two seconds. That's all that stands between running away and being a victim. *Two seconds.*"

Her heart started pounding. She'd swear his voice, quiet as it'd been against her ear, vibrated around the empty apartment that he was now occupying. She needed a moment to remember how to breathe. Closing her eyes, she leaned into him a bit more than necessary as his heat enveloped her. She didn't lift her lids again until the moist heat of his breath tickled her cheek. He lowered his hands and gently pushed her away and she faced him.

Then he reached for her. She locked her hands together,

spun her back to him, and shoved her elbow down with all her force, jerking free from his hold.

"Good," he said from behind her. "Again."

She did, and then did it again several more times and probably would have done it several more, but her cell phone pinged and she stopped to read the message. "They're here," she told him, and a giddy smile spread across her face. She hurried toward the door and down the stairs, reaching the bottom just as the hardware-store deliverymen lifted the door on the truck. Watching them pull the panels from the back made her want to squeal.

"In here," Daniel ordered, and she let him. He was the one who would be installing the wainscoting; she'd let him handle the process of delivery as well. But once the load was sitting in the back of the kitchen, she signed the paperwork and went inside to admire the wood.

"On a scale of one to ten, how big of a dork does it make me that standing here looking at these flimsy pieces of pressed wood makes me so incredibly happy?"

"Eleven," Scott called from the grill.

She ignored him. His naturally gloomy mood wasn't going to overshadow hers. This was a step—a rather large step, in her mind—toward the facelift she'd been wanting to give the café. She couldn't wait to see the wainscoting on the walls.

"It doesn't," Daniel said as he glanced at his watch. "Just about closing time. What do you say we get started?"

"We?"

"Your help is needed on this one, Miss Jenna."

While it was easy enough to put the wainscoting up on his own, Daniel liked the idea of letting Jenna help. He had a few reasons, but he focused on the one that involved giving her back some pride in her café by having her do some of the hands-on work of repairing it. He was ignoring the reasons that kept her close to him for just a bit longer. He wouldn't keep her long. She'd worked all day and dark circles were starting to form under her eyes, but he wasn't quite ready to face how empty the café felt when she left him alone.

"We need to pull the booths out so I can get to the wall." He handed her a screwdriver and showed her where to find the brackets that secured the seating to the wall. While he pulled tables out she removed screws, and then he went behind her and pulled the booths back enough to give them room to work. He'd measured and marked the walls the night before when he'd pulled the paneling, so he was already ahead of the process.

Within a few minutes, Jenna was trailing behind as he carried a panel of pressed wood to the alley. He had her hold the board as he measured and marked it, and then prepped Charlie's jigsaw. Not long after, she was helping him press it against the wall. "Still level?"

"Yep."

"Hold it while I drive a few nails in." The gun *thunked* as it shot finishing nails through the board and into the café's studs. "That's it. First board's up."

She stepped back as he set the gun aside. Brushing his hands, he stood and faced her, pausing at the way she had her hands over her mouth and tears had filled her eyes.

"This will look better after I give it a light sanding and add finish."

She shook her head. "It already looks beautiful."

She sniffed and he grinned and maybe stood a bit taller.

"I never would have gotten this done without you, Daniel. I couldn't possibly have asked Marcus to do this and anyone else would charge an arm and a leg. Thank you." She put her hand on his arm and held his gaze. "I mean it. Thank you. This place is already looking so much better."

He cleared his throat as he wiped his hands on his pants again, pretending to brush away dust or glue or...whatever it was that was stirring inside him. Oh, right. Pride. That feeling was pride. He hadn't felt that in some time, but seeing her so happy and knowing he had a hand in making the smile on her face made him feel proud. Made him want to rebuild the entire damn building. "You're welcome," he said before moving around her to get the next board.

They followed the same process—measure, cut, glue, nail— and then Jenna would stand back and smile and Daniel would have to take a deep breath to keep himself grounded.

When the last board was put in place, she laughed. "Oh my god, Daniel. Look at that. It's amazing."

There was that damned warmth expanding in his chest again. "And it's not done yet."

"What's left?"

"I need to fill where the nails went in and give it a quick sanding before I put the varnish on. I think that'll keep until tomorrow night, though," he said, looking at his watch. "It's getting a bit late to paint tonight. The surface will be sticky when you open. Don't want to ruin someone's clothes. Or overcome anyone with fumes."

She nodded her agreement. "So what do you need me to do?"

"Go to bed." He nodded toward the kitchen when she looked at him, clearly confused. "You're exhausted. I can handle the rest of this."

After a few seconds longer of looking at the latest upgrade to the café, she sighed. "Okay. I'm going to bed." She lingered, still staring at the wall. "I'm really glad you're here, Daniel."

He swallowed hard, surprised at her words. "So am I, Jenna." He waited until he heard the kitchen door open before following her. He didn't want her to know he was watching, but suspected she wasn't completely unaware. He focused on brushing the sawdust off Charlie's tools while she walked up the stairs. Once she was inside her apartment, safe behind her door, he locked the tools in the box in the bed of the truck and went back inside.

He filled a cup of coffee and stood back, as she had done, admiring the work they'd done as her words played over in his mind.

"I'm really glad you're here, Daniel."

When the hell had anyone ever said that to him and meant it? As he stood there, staring at the damn wall, his need to make this café the best it could be for Jenna became his new mission. This was no longer just a project to pass time or to keep his mind from focusing on how shitty his life had become.

Saving this café was his new purpose in life. His only purpose in life.

Well, that, and bringing a smile to Jenna's face as often as he could.

CHAPTER NINE

*S*eeing the café back in order took Jenna's breath away, but seeing Daniel leaning against the wall, sound asleep in one of the booths, made her chuckle. He'd put the seating and tables back in place and swept the floor clean. The truck was no longer in the alley, so at some point he'd returned the vehicle and presumably walked back only to fall asleep, despite the coffee cup sitting on the table beside him.

She eased to the booth where he was slumped against the wall and took the cup. She'd let him rest while she made breakfast. She practically hummed as she tossed hash browns on the griddle and cracked and scrambled eggs for omelets. She started a fresh pot of coffee and served up two heaping plates. She slid the plates onto the table where he'd dozed off and called out to him, smiling when he didn't even stir.

"Hey, I made breakfast."

He still didn't respond, so she put her hand to his knee and gave him a gentle shake. The amusement she'd found in him sleeping faded the instant he gripped her wrist and twisted.

How many times had he told her two seconds was all the reaction time she had? A dozen or more? He hadn't been kidding. She tried to knock his hand away, but the way he turned her arm, her body had no choice but to follow.

She yelped, and his hold on her eased, but it was too late. She'd already gone too far into the motion. Starbursts exploded behind her eyelids when her forehead cracked on the table edge as she dropped to her knees to ease the pain in her arm.

"Oh, shit. Jenna." He sat beside her and pried her hand from her head. "God. I'm sorry. I'm so sorry."

"My fault," she said around her grimace. "I scared you. Am I bleeding?"

"No," he whispered.

She blinked a few times as the pain started to spread and throb. He sat before her, guilt and shame and a hundred other emotions playing across his face.

"I'm sorry," he said under his breath again. He dragged his hand over his hair and she grabbed for him.

Gripping his hand with hers, she waited for him to look at her. "That was my fault. I scared you. I should have known better."

"No. I should have known better. I don't belong here."

She widened her eyes. "Daniel."

"I hurt you."

"I fell."

"Because I hurt you."

Her heart ached at the horror in his eyes. She put her hands to his face, forcing him to look at her. She realized that probably didn't help when his gaze immediately went to what was likely a ping-pong-ball-sized knot by now. "Look at me," she said in as soothing of a voice as she could manage given the ache rapidly spreading across her forehead. "I didn't think before grabbing you. I know better now. I won't do that again."

He exhaled harshly. "I should go."

"No." She stroked his face like she would a child. "This was an accident. Take a breath. Daniel, take a deep breath."

He did. And he let it out slowly before finally focusing on her eyes instead of her injury.

"I need you to do something for me, okay?"

"What?"

"There's one of those gel ice packs in the freezer. On the door. Wrap it in a towel and bring it to me."

He hesitated before standing. As he did, he slowly pulled her to her feet and helped her sit in the booth. She exhaled a deep breath as soon as he rushed toward the kitchen. *Holy shit. Holy shit.* She wasn't about to let on to him how much that had scared the crap out of her, but *holy shit*.

A few seconds later, he was pressing the pack into her hands. "Do you need to go to the ER?"

She smiled as she pressed the pack to her forehead. "No. But I'll need some aspirin as soon as I get food in my stomach."

His lack of response caused her to open her eyes and look at him.

He was clearly beating himself up. She meant what she'd said though. She was more to blame than he was. She knew his history, knew that he'd spent years on active duty. Trying to wake him like that had been stupid. Putting her free hand to one of his, she squeezed it. "I'm sorry."

"Don't apologize to me, Jenna. I hurt you." He shook his head. "I was so stupid to think this time would be any different."

"This is different."

When he looked up, the storm in his eyes surprised her. "I'm dangerous. I've told myself since finding my way into your alley that I'd protect you. That I'd never hurt you. But look at you. Look at what I did to you. This is why Charlie's wife didn't want me in her house, Jenna. She knew what I was capable of and she was scared that I'd react to a situation like that and hurt her."

"Hey," she snapped as he started talking faster, getting more upset with each word. "Daniel. I won't do that again, okay?"

"Yeah. Lesson learned. But what if you walk into a room and I'm not expecting you? What if you don't know I'm there and you startle me?" He ran his hands over his hair again. "I'm not cut out for this. I've spent too much time living on edge to not automatically attack. I'd never forgive myself if… I'll never forgive myself for this, but this could have been so much worse. I have to leave, Jenna."

"Stop," she ordered when he started to slide out of the booth.

He didn't. He walked away from her and his breakfast. She

dropped the ice pack and rushed around him as he neared the back door, putting herself between him and the exit.

"You're not leaving."

"Jenna."

Leaning against the door, she cocked a brow at him when he reached for the knob. Covering it with her hand, she waited until he met her gaze. "You're not giving up, Daniel."

"I could have killed you."

"I could have killed you."

He creased his brow.

"You were sound asleep. I could have shot you. I could have stabbed you. I could have poisoned your omelet."

"Don't be stupid," he said on a frustrated sigh.

"*You* don't be stupid. Where are you going to go?"

"It doesn't matter."

"It matters to me."

"Why?" he demanded.

"I don't know," she said just as sternly in return. "Because you've helped me. Because you don't treat me like an idiot. Because you seem to respect me."

"I do respect you." His tone softened, easing the tension between them.

"Well, I respect you, too. And I understand how hard you're trying. And how hard it is to start over when you've lost everything. I know what it's like to lose every ounce of pride you have. I know running away is so much easier than fighting to start over. But you can't keep running away."

"I can't keep hurting people."

She nodded. "If you'd known that was me, would have you reacted like that?"

"Of course not."

"Of course not. I trust you. Daniel, I trust you. I do. You've earned my trust. You've shown me that I can believe in someone again. I believe in *you*. I know that sounds trite, I don't mean it to, but I see how hard you're working and I believe you can overcome the things that are holding you back. It won't be easy, but I want to help you."

"At what expense, Jenna?" He frowned. "The price is too high."

He put his hands to her arms to push her aside, but she stepped into him and wrapped her arms around his neck. He stood, unmoving, and she expected him to pull away from her, but after a few tense moments, he wrapped his arms around her waist and held her even closer.

"Don't give up," she whispered in his ear. "Please."

He buried his face in her shoulder, clinging to her, and she could have sworn she felt a sob wrack his body ever so slightly. She hugged him tighter and had to wonder who was comforting whom. His arms, wrapped around her, felt like salve soothing the illogical fear that he was going to leave her. She wasn't sure how long they stood like that before he eased his hold, and she leaned back.

His eyes were sad, and she couldn't stop herself from putting her palm to his cheek.

"You've been working too hard," she whispered. "Staying up all night and only sleeping half the morning to catch up."

"I'm used to that."

"Well, you need to take tonight off. Get some rest. I can put the varnish on in no time at all," she said before he could protest. "I want you to sleep."

He pressed his lips together and nodded.

Lowering her hand from his face, she bit her lip. "Stay here. Don't move." She rushed into the dining room, grabbed his breakfast from the table, and dumped the omelet and hash browns into a to-go container, and then filled a cup with coffee and picked up disposable utensils. She was glad to see him still standing here, head down, when she returned. "Take this upstairs. Eat and get some sleep."

"Thanks."

"I'm going to bring some lunch up to you today. About two?"

"Don't want me near your customers?"

"I suspect you're going to lie awake thinking of all the reasons you should leave. I don't want to have to talk you out of that in front of my customers." She grinned.

He met her with half a smile of his own before disappearing out the kitchen door. Leaning against it, she rolled her head back. Pain bounced around her brain. Lifting her hand, she gently touched the knot on her head. "Oh, man," she moaned, knowing she'd spend the day reassuring everyone she served that she was fine and hoping that her brother didn't stop in for lunch today. If Marcus knew what had happened, he'd have freaked.

8h

Jenna was right. Daniel had barely slept. He'd barely eaten. The omelet was delicious, but he couldn't stomach what he'd done. Every time he closed his eyes, he saw Jenna sitting on the floor with a knot on her head. He hoped she'd iced the injury and taken aspirin like she said she would. Even so, he knew she'd have a hell of a headache from the way her head had cracked against the table.

He's a loose cannon.

That's what he'd overheard Lisa telling Charlie.

Who knows what he could do!

He had finished packing his bag before Charlie even knocked on the guest room door to ask him to leave. Lisa had been right to want him gone. Charlie had been right to let him go. And if he were half the man he pretended to be, he'd have left before Jenna came upstairs to talk him into staying.

Closing his eyes, he let the image of her curled on the floor holding her head be replaced by the feel of her arms around him and the scent of her filling his senses. He'd never really had a serious relationship. He was married to the army. That was a relationship he understood, one he thought he could never screw up right up until he did. He didn't know much about women or what it meant to really care about someone other than his mother.

So the calming sensation that thinking of Jenna brought to him was new. He wasn't foolish enough to think he was in love.

They didn't know each other well enough for that mess. But he felt something and he felt it strongly. Something that he'd never felt before. Part of him wanted to pull her inside of him and protect her from the world. The other part of him wanted to see her out in the world taking care of everyone the way she took care of him. She had so much to give but he didn't think she realized that about herself. He wanted to make her see how much happiness he brought to her customers, even if she just took care of them for an hour or so of their day. He wanted to push her into the sunlight and watch her shine. But he also wanted to lock her away so no one could ever take that shine away from her.

He didn't understand this contradictory mix of emotions. He was used to the black-and-white order of military life. The colors she brought to his life were confusing.

He also didn't understand how one hug from her had nearly undone him. She'd wrapped her arms around him and the urge to break down had almost overwhelmed him. She'd made him feel that being weak was okay. That maybe he didn't have to get through this life alone. That was just about enough to bring him to his knees.

"Jesus, I'm so fucked up," he muttered, rolling over. Looking at his watch, he decided he'd never sleep now. He took a quick shower and put on clean clothes. He'd have to get to the laundromat sooner rather than later. Then again, maybe he should save his coins for buying food off the dollar menu of local fast food joints.

As much as he didn't want Jenna to come and talk him into staying, he wanted her to convince him that he should. He couldn't imagine not being here. In this empty apartment. Above her rundown café. Being in this place, with this woman, brought a sense of belonging he wasn't ready to give up. Another thing about the woman he didn't understand.

He'd just finished putting his dirty clothes into his pack when she knocked on the door. He opened it and gestured for her to come in. She stopped just inside the door and looked around. As she did, he looked at where she'd bumped her head. She had her hair styled to cover the right side of her forehead. He frowned and lightly traced his fingers over her head to push the strands aside.

"It's fine," she said despite the dark-purple mark that was surrounded by a slightly lighter oval bruise and a still-visible knot. "Come with me," she said, and headed down the stairs again.

He followed her to her apartment door and held the food containers she'd brought up as she dug her key out of her pocket. He'd never stepped foot inside her place and the idea of it made him a bit nervous. Seeing her outside of the café seemed odd. Like a kid seeing a schoolteacher at a restaurant and realizing there was more to her than what he'd seen in the classroom.

She held the door open, and he stepped inside. The layout was just like his—wide open with a kitchen in a corner and one door that led to the bathroom. Only she had furniture. He entered the area that she had sectioned off for a living room as he scanned her apartment, and then quickly turned away from the full-sized bed that was against one wall. Somehow that felt like a violation of her privacy.

Returning his focus to the cream-colored walls and the area rug with a plush brown couch and matching chair that faced the television attached to the wall, he thought that even though the room was open, she'd made it feel cozy and warm. The area suited her. Perfectly.

"Over there." She gestured.

He crossed the room and set the containers on a small round table in the kitchen area and immediately went to wash his hands in the sink. By the time he sat, she was pulling cups from the carrier she'd brought up.

"Looked like your bag was packed."

"I was going to go to the laundromat."

"Use the washer and dryer in the café after closing tonight."

He started to argue, but she lifted her brow at him. "Okay. Thanks. Lunch looks amazing."

"It is amazing. I made it."

He smiled and dug into the gravy-covered mashed potatoes.

"Did you sleep?"

"No."

"Didn't think you would."

His food suddenly seemed less appetizing. "I can't stop thinking about this morning."

"I've been thinking about it, too."

His heart plummeted to his stomach and the potatoes in his

mouth lost their appeal. He met her gaze, expecting to see guilt or pity or anger. But she was looking at him as she always did—with warmth and kindness. "You want me to leave?"

"No. Of course not. I told you earlier that I don't want you to leave. Daniel, I scared you. You reacted. But you're right. It could happen again, even if we are both careful. Or it could happen to someone else at the café or the store or just walking down the street. This reaction that you have to being startled or your need to protect someone—it could be dangerous. I know you don't want to hurt anybody."

"No. I don't."

She bit her lip. "I made some calls earlier." She leaned over and pulled a piece of paper from her back pocket and slid it to him.

He opened it to a clinic name and phone number in her slanted handwriting.

"Their services are income-based. I called and let them know a little about your situation. They have programs to cover the cost of counseling."

He inhaled slowly before cutting his gaze to her. "I don't need a shrink."

"Daniel," she said softly, obviously knowing she was treading on sensitive ground, "you were discharged from the army—political reasons aside—for losing your tempter. You've lost three jobs, from your account in the kitchen, for losing your temper. You're terrified of losing your temper again. You need to take steps to learn how to control yourself." She simply held his stare for a few heartbeats before nodding. "I won't push. That's not my place. If you decide, call them. They'll help you."

"I'm not crazy."

She chuckled. "We're all crazy in our own ways. I bought this café out of spite. Not a damn moment of planning went into this. I just... I was pissed at my husband for walking out on me. At my friend for betraying me. At the judge for screwing me over. At myself for giving away all my money. At the world for not turning my way. It was insane to buy this café. It was rash and irresponsible."

"It turned out okay."

She nodded. "It's getting better. But only because I finally accepted the help that I needed to make it better. *Your* help. And I want to help you in return. But your problems run deeper than my battered pride. I can only do so much. I'll do it for as long as you'll let me, but I can only heal the surface wounds. Nothing you do is going to take the edge off that anger you've been carrying all these years until you jump in and deal with it. You know that, don't you?"

His appetite was officially gone. He set his fork down and sighed.

"I won't bring it up again, but would you please just hang on to that number? Just in case you decide to use it."

He nodded and stared at his food. The idea of telling some headshrinker about his problems didn't sit well at all. Some pansy-ass, touchy-feely session wasn't going to erase the memories of seeing his mom crying and wiping blood from her nose. Or the shame of hiding instead of trying to protect her. He didn't need to revisit all that to know he had anger issues. He had never had to control his anger before. The army had been a good outlet for all that rage. Now that he didn't have that, he just had to find a way to reconcile his fury. He could do it. He knew he could.

And it wasn't like he ever took it out on someone who didn't deserve it. Asshole wife-beaters. Attempted rapists. They deserved his fury. But then his eyes drifted to the strands covering Jenna's forehead in an attempt to hide her injury. His mother used tricks to hide her bruises, too. Long sleeves at the height of summer. Sunglasses indoors. Layer upon layer of makeup.

A sense of shame that he'd never felt before washed over him. He'd done that to Jenna. No, he hadn't meant to, but wasn't that what his father had always said? He didn't mean to lash out. He didn't mean to hurt anyone. He didn't mean to lose his temper.

Fuck. Charlie was right. Daniel was just like his dad.

He couldn't be that man. He couldn't have Jenna fear him. That'd break him. That'd kill what was left of his soul.

He cleared his throat. "Can, uh, can I use your phone?"

She gave him that supportive smile of hers as she slid her cell phone across the table. He hesitated only for a moment before dialing. He looked down so he wouldn't have to see her face as he answered questions, but when it came time to give an address, he looked at her desperately.

She rattled off the café address and phone number, which he repeated. When he hung up, he was exhausted. Emotionally. Mentally. Physically. He sank down in the chair and put her phone on the table.

"They squeezed me in tomorrow."

"I can drive you."

"I can walk. I'd rather walk."

"If you change your mind…"

He closed his food container. No way he could eat now. His stomach was tied in knots and turned inside out just thinking about what he'd done. His father would mock him. His CO would tell him he wasn't fit to lead. But when he looked at Jenna, she looked pleased. And supportive. And approving.

And somehow that was all that mattered.

She covered his hand with hers and gently pulled him with her across her apartment to the sofa. "Lie down."

He simply stared at the furniture.

"When was the last time you slept on something other than the ground?"

"A while."

"So lie down and get some sleep."

He stretched out while she grabbed a blanket from the chair next to the sofa and then draped it over him and sat on the edge of the couch. The surprising hope that she'd stretch out next to him filled him, but she just looked down at him.

"I didn't think you'd actually call."

"Me either. But I…I remember how my mother used to look

at my dad. She lived in fear, never knowing what to expect. She was always on eggshells. Always careful what she said and did. I don't ever want you to look at me like that, Jenna. I gotta fix this so you don't ever look at me like that."

"You'll fix it," she whispered. "Everything's going to be okay, Daniel. Just close your eyes and sleep now."

He inhaled deeply as he felt exhaustion taking over his mind. Her scent was on the blanket and soothed his anxiety as he floated into darkness, a spark of hope lighting inside him. Maybe, just maybe, everything really would be okay this time.

CHAPTER TEN

*J*enna eased her apartment door open, knowing that if she pushed too far, the hinges would creak. She poked her head in, confirming that Daniel was still asleep on the sofa. Not wanting to wake him, she slipped through the barely open door, slowly turned the locks, and slid the chain into place. Then she tiptoed to the bathroom and turned on the shower and stripped down, testing the water before easing under the stream. She sighed as the heat hit her muscles. Forget waiting tables and scrubbing floors—trying to maneuver around the booths so she could get varnish on the wall had been the real workout.

After drying off, she wiped the condensation from the mirror and looked at the bruise on her forehead. The deep purple had grown darker over the day but at least the swelling had gone down, making the wound a bit less obvious. She'd have to pin her hair over that side of her forehead for a good week or so, she expected.

Even with her attempt at hiding the goose egg, a few people had asked what had happened. She'd admitted to hitting her head on the edge of the table, but left out the physical assault by a homeless veteran part and implied that she was bending to pick something up. A little white lie to save herself a whole lot of explaining. Thankfully her brother hadn't visited today, but she usually saw him and Annie several times a week, so her luck wouldn't last. She didn't know if Marcus would buy her tale, but she wasn't about to tell him the truth.

He was already suspicious of her handyman. If he knew Daniel had anger issues that had inadvertently led to her smacking her head, he wouldn't rest until Daniel was long gone. Then he'd spend the rest of his life reminding Jenna how dumb it had been to hire him in the first place.

She dragged a brush through her still-wet hair and brushed and flossed her teeth before carefully turning the knob and opening the bathroom door, listening for Daniel's rhythmic breathing. She muffled a chuckle when he snorted. With nothing but the moonlight to guide her, she moved to the kitchen, filled a glass of water, and carried it with her to bed.

She'd slid between the cool sheets and fluffed her pillow before she even considered the fact that she'd showered and crawled into bed while a strange man slept on her sofa. God. Maybe she was as naïve as Peter had accused her of being. She rolled onto her side and looked toward the sofa, though she could only see the basic outline in the dark room. As she stared, she did a mental check and decided, no, there was nothing about the situation that made her feel unsafe.

She swore that she'd just closed her eyes when the damned alarm went off. She smacked the phone without looking, pressing the button to put an end to the old Fleetwood Mac song she woke up to every morning. When she took a deep breath in an attempt to work up the desire to get out of bed, her senses filled with the scents of coffee and...was that cinnamon rolls?

Forcing her eyes open, she lifted her head enough to look at her kitchen. Daniel eased the oven door open and pulled a tray out and yes, the sweet smell grew stronger. He'd baked the cinnamon rolls that had been sitting in her fridge, calling her name for the last three weeks. Every time she thought about baking them, she reminded herself that she didn't need all the empty calories, but right now, that was the thing she needed most.

And coffee. He'd brewed coffee in the rarely used pot that sat on her counter.

Rolling onto her side, she curled so she could watch him. She smiled when he cursed as he pried a roll off the cookie sheet and then dropped it onto a plate. After the second time he burned his fingers, she said, "There's a spatula in the second drawer."

He glanced back. "I got it." Then he cursed and rubbed his fingers again, squeezed the packet of icing over the plate, and headed in her direction, nabbing a cup off the counter as he went.

She pushed herself to sit as he set the coffee on her nightstand and held the plate out to her. She couldn't help the grin that spread across her lips. "Breakfast in bed?"

"It's not an omelet and hash browns, but it's the best I could do."

"It's perfect. Thank you." She leaned against the headboard and accepted a roll. She bit into it and moaned her appreciation. "Delicious. How'd you sleep?"

"Like a rock." He looked around, but the closest chair was several feet away.

"Sit." She nodded toward her bed.

He hesitated before easing down on the edge of her bed. "I hope you don't mind me making breakfast. I was fidgety, but didn't want to leave. I had no way of locking your door behind me."

"Are you kidding?" she asked around the mouthful. "I can't remember the last time someone cooked for me." She smiled when he did. She was quickly learning that little compliments went a long way with him—not in an egotistical way, just rebuilding the confidence that too often seemed chipped beyond repair.

"Did you get the varnish up?"

"I did. Should be dry by now."

"We should open some windows. That stuff smells worse than paint."

She touched her forehead when she noticed him staring at her bruise. "How is it?"

"Worse."

"Well, wounds tend to get worse before getting better." She focused on picking up her coffee as she said, "Remember that when you start counseling today." She dared to cast a glance his way.

He sat, staring at a cinnamon roll.

"If you need to talk about anything," she said, "anything at all, I'm here and not judging."

He nodded before stuffing the roll in his mouth. He put the plate on her nightstand before standing. "You should get ready for work. I'll see you later."

And with that, he unlocked all the deadbolts on her door and disappeared.

sh

Daniel dragged his hand over his face at the sound of a soft knock on the door. Jenna. A glance at his watch told him why she was knocking on his door. He hadn't gone down to the café for lunch. She was probably wondering why.

He took a few cleansing breaths before opening the door. "Hey."

"I wasn't sure if you were here," she said. "Hungry?"

"Sure." He opened the door and stepped aside.

"I can just leave this if you want to be alone."

Funny thing was that he did right up until he saw her

standing there. "Actually, I wouldn't mind company. That is, if you don't mind standing."

"I actually have a lead on some furniture."

"I don't want a handout."

"It's not for you." She put the bag she'd carried upstairs onto the counter and turned to face him. "Eventually, I'll rent it as partially furnished." She shrugged as if that had been her plan all along.

He wasn't going to argue. It'd be great to have a chair. Or a bed. He'd slept like a rock on her couch the night before. He estimated that he'd gotten a solid twelve hours' sleep before waking up to the sound of her snoring softly. He grinned as he recalled the sound. Not obnoxious snoring, just the heavy breathing of a body completely worn out.

After a few minutes, he had gotten up, used the bathroom, and washed his face. He'd considered going to his apartment, but he had no way to lock the door behind him and damned if he'd leave the door open. Instead, he'd quietly made coffee and sat at the table drinking and watching the lump in the bed, fighting the urge to curl up next to her. Something told him she wouldn't find the same kind of comfort from his holding her that he would.

She set the last container on the counter and met his gaze. "I don't expect you to tell me how it went, but...you did go, right?"

He shifted, recalling how humiliating it'd been explaining to a stranger why he was sitting there seeking help. "Yeah, I went."

She didn't press, but he thought she likely wanted to know more. Maybe he just wanted to share more.

"I don't think it's going to help."

"You can't know that after one session, Daniel. The first session is always awkward. You know you're just trying to feel each other out and let the counselor know the deal. It'll take a few times before you feel comfortable enough to really let him...her?"

"Her."

"It'll take time before you are ready to really let her in on what's going on."

"You're speaking from experience?"

"I went to counseling for months after my divorce. I mean, Peter left me with some pretty deep insecurities that still bite me in the ass when I least expect it. I'm still working on that. It takes a long time to heal. Don't expect miracles, okay?"

He sighed as he opened the container. "Meatloaf? It's not Tuesday."

She smiled. "Well, someone once told me that meatloaf was your favorite. I thought today might be a good day for you to have your favorite."

He nodded. "Thank you."

"I meant what I said this morning. I'm here if you want to talk."

Taking a breath, he let it out slowly. "Not right now, but I'll keep your offer in mind. But since you're here, I stopped by Carson's on the way home and picked up some paint samples. I think you should consider something similar to what you have in your apartment. It really makes the space seem even larger." He spread out the samples he'd picked up and smiled when she pointed to the same one he had liked best. "I think two gallons would be enough. Whenever you're ready to tackle this place."

"I can splurge for some paint if you're willing to slap it on the walls."

He nodded and grabbed her binder of plans for the café, intending to keep her mind and the topic of their conversation off his problems.

CHAPTER ELEVEN

*J*enna smiled as a man sat at the counter. "Good afternoon."

"Ma'am."

"Something to drink?" she asked as she slid a menu to him. She sensed something off about him. The way he watched her— not looked at her, but *watched* her—as he ordered a diet soda set her on edge. She liked to take a few minutes to chat with her customers, especially ones she'd not met before, but she didn't feel much like trying to make that hometown connection with this man. She'd never met him, but he seemed to be judging her.

She focused on filling a glass for him and then set it on the counter and pulled a straw from her apron. "Know what you want?"

"How's the meatloaf?"

"Best in town," she said with a warm smile. "Or so I like to think. Mashed potatoes and a roll?"

"Sounds good."

She stuck his ticket to the order wheel and grabbed a coffeepot from the burner to top off various cups and check on the diners. All the while, she kept an eye on the man at the counter. She wasn't sure she'd ever seen anyone as interested in the café itself as he seemed to be. He looked up, his eyes traveling the length of the wall and counters and then moving on to look around the dining room. As if he were memorizing every inch of the building.

Or making a note of the location of her security cameras?

She returned the coffeepot and went into the kitchen, where she spun the wheel until she found the man's order. "Fill this right away," she said to Scott. "I want that guy out of here. He's making me nervous."

She left him to it and went back to the dining room to see what the stranger was up to now.

He'd grabbed a newspaper while she was gone, but as soon as she reappeared, she felt his gaze on her. Maybe all Daniel's training was getting to her. All his warnings about how vulnerable she was had started eating away at her confidence. Or maybe this was the moment he'd been warning her about. It certainly felt like this guy was casing her café.

Scott hit the bell. Jenna was relieved to see it was the meatloaf that she'd requested he hurry to put together. She slid the plate onto the counter and nodded to the half-empty soda. "Refill?"

"Please," he said, staring at her with his dark eyes.

She stuck the glass under the dispenser, hoping he would eat and leave without incident. As she returned the drink to the customer, she even debated running upstairs to see if Daniel was up yet. He didn't usually appear for lunch until a bit later in the afternoon, but she was confident that if asked, he'd come sit in the diner, just to keep an eye on the man.

The temptation was strong, but so was her determination to stop letting the men in her life swoop in and save her. She was aware of this man. He was on her radar. She pulled the order pad from her apron and started jotting notes in case she needed it later. *Brown hair, mid-fifties, moustache, overweight...*

"Ma'am?"

She looked at the man she'd been describing on the pad and smiled. "Everything okay?"

"You're the owner?"

"Yeah." She slipped the pad back in her pocket and closed the distance between them. "Something wrong with your lunch?"

"No." He offered her what seemed to be the first genuine smile she'd seen from him since he'd entered. "Actually, I think you're right. Best in town. Don't tell my wife that." He chuckled.

She gave him a light laugh, but her sense of unease hadn't lightened. There was some underlying purpose to his sitting at her counter eating meatloaf, and she suspected he was about to get to it. Her nerves sizzled with a wave of anxiety.

"I can see why Daniel thinks highly of you."

She leaned back at the mentioned of her new friend.

"I'm his uncle. Charlie Burke."

Ah, he hadn't been casing the café. He'd been judging Daniel's work.

She accepted the hand that Charlie held out to her. "Jenna Reid. Thank you for letting Daniel borrow your truck and tools to help me out. I appreciate it."

"Well, I appreciate you giving him a place to stay. And food to eat."

"He's earned it," she said. Daniel hadn't been completely open about his relationship with his uncle, but she suspected it wasn't a solid one. As sensitive as Daniel was about feeling like he was taking advantage of her, she wanted to make sure Charlie knew that wasn't the case. "He's done amazing work on the café."

He nodded and looked around again. "He painted."

"And the wainscoting and fixed the tables. He's been incredibly helpful."

Charlie kept nodding, slowly and thoughtfully.

"You have something to say to that," she said.

"You seem like a nice person."

"I like to think so." She didn't mean to sound defensive, but she had been from the moment he'd walked in.

"Look, Danny...he has problems."

"Anger issues. He's told me."

"He said he's doing the work at night? When you're closed?"

"Yes."

He gave that thoughtful nod again. "Are you ever here alone with him?"

And there it was. What he'd come here to say. She drew a breath. "Mr. Burke—"

"Charlie."

"*Mr. Burke*. Daniel has told me about his past. His discharge and trouble holding a job. I assure you, if I felt the slightest bit threatened by him, he wouldn't be working with me to improve my building, let alone living in it. He's been nothing but kind and helpful."

"I don't mean to offend," he said more gently. "But I know Danny a lot better than you."

Taking a breath, she swallowed before speaking. "Maybe you don't know him nearly as well as you think." Biting her lip, she debated before walking around the counter and sitting on the stool next to him. "We all have things in our lives that we wish we could change. That we'd like to take back. If those things are constantly thrown in our faces, how are we supposed to ever grow and learn and move on? He's suffered the consequences of his actions, and he deserves a chance to rebuild his life. I know you tried to give him that chance. I don't think you could be any more upset that it didn't work out than Daniel is. I think letting you down hurt his pride even more than losing his career. You gave him a chance and he blew it and he knows that. So maybe this will be the chance that works out."

"He give you that bruise?"

She instinctively touched her forehead. "I hit my head on a table."

"How'd you manage that?"

She scoffed. "I dropped my magic wand. Look, you have your reasons for giving up on Daniel, and I have my reasons for standing by him."

"You seem like a real nice lady. I don't want him taking advantage of you."

"He's not." She gestured around her. "He's working for his room and board. If anything, I owe him. I've had estimates done for the work he's doing. I know what this would cost me if I hired a contractor. That's *why* I hadn't hired a contractor. Listen, it's nice of you to be concerned about me, but I'm fine. So is Daniel. He's working through some things, but he's fine. Lunch is on the house. A thank-you for letting Daniel use your supplies."

"Ms. Reid," he called as she stood. "I didn't know until things got bad, but Danny's dad used to take out an awful lot of frustration on my sister. She made all kinds of excuses for him. She always had a way to justify what he'd done. When she was gone, I'm pretty sure Danny got the brunt of that anger. He never said so, but his father never remarried and he wasn't the kind to *not* take his anger out on someone."

Jenna's heart ached for Daniel. "All the more reason to show him some compassion, don't you think?"

"Listen to me," Charlie said as he leaned a bit closer. "That kind of childhood sticks with a man. Shapes who he becomes whether he wants it to or not. Maybe that bump on your head was an accident. This time. But it's a hell of a cycle to break once it starts. I tried to save my sister, but she was so determined to help that man. Excuse after excuse, reason after reason. I don't pretend to understand why, but I do know that she always thought she could fix him if she just loved him enough. But nothing she ever did was enough. I don't want to see another good woman fall into that cycle. Find another cause, Ms. Reid. Danny's not going to be worth the trouble."

"I do appreciate your concern, but Daniel's worth isn't for you to decide. Have a good day, Mr. Burke."

Daniel leaned back to stretch out his back muscles. All the windows in the apartment meant less paint, but more bending and kneeling and carefully tracing the window edges. He was starting to feel the tension of such detailed work.

"Wow," Jenna said, coming in through his open door. "Look at this place."

He turned and met her smile with one of his own. He found it impossible not to smile when she was beaming like that.

"You are one serious painting machine. It'd take me days to do all this."

"Well," he said, rolling his stiff shoulders, "I am a professional."

She giggled and held up two food containers. "Ready for dinner?"

"Sure am." He set his brush aside and went to wash up. "How's your day been?"

"Uh. So-so."

"Why just so-so?" he asked, drying his hands. He joined her at the counter.

"I'm sure you've noticed Scott isn't the most helpful cooking assistant. He's really trying my patience lately."

"What's he doing?"

She glanced up and he was certain he saw her debating what to tell him. He wasn't sure if that was because she was worried he'd pummel the kid or she just didn't want to share her problems with him.

"He's really giving me attitude lately. I let it go for so long because, honestly, I couldn't see myself staying open much longer. Now things are looking up a bit and I'm struggling with the decision to replace him. I've asked him several times to pick up the pace on filling orders and warned him about his attitude. He snaps at everyone, including me, and I'm his boss. It's not the best environment in the kitchen when he's there."

"Well, he's got a shitty work ethic. That's all I'm going to say."

She chuckled. "And you didn't have to say that much. I know he does. Part of that is my fault for letting him get away with it."

"That's just it. If he were worth what you are paying him, there wouldn't be anything for you to reprimand. I think if you replace him with someone who is willing to work for the money and respect you and the job, you'll realize how much of a slacker that kid really is."

She blew a raspberry. "I'm sure you are right. I just hate the idea of firing him."

"Think he'll give you problems?"

"Undoubtedly. But I just need to do it. He tries me at every turn these days."

"Want me to handle it?"

"No. My staff; my responsibility. Thanks, though."

"Well, let me know if you need me to be around. I'd be happy to glower at him while you put him in his place."

She laughed. "I believe that." She cleared her throat as she dug into her dinner. "I don't know if now is the best time to tell you this, but your uncle stopped by the café today."

She lifted her eyes to his, and his chest tightened with anxiety.

"I probably don't have to guess what he wanted."

"He told me to be careful around you."

He dropped his fork and let out some of his frustration on a breath.

"I told him I'd been taking self-defense classes and could totally take you if it came to it."

She grinned slowly, and he felt his nerves settle in the way they did whenever she smiled.

"Actually, I told him that I know all about your problems and I thanked him for his concern, but let him know you were working on things."

"Did he drop it after that?"

"No." Her playfulness faded a bit. "He said that you're pretty scarred from your childhood. He said he doesn't know for certain, but he suspects that after your mom passed away, you became the target of your dad's anger."

He looked down at his dinner. Why did she always have to start on these deep conversations when he was trying to enjoy his damn dinner?

"You know, other than falling into Peter's trap, my life has been pretty vanilla. My parents were older when they had me, so they were pretty relaxed and established. We took our annual summer vacations. Yellowstone, Grand Canyon, Gettysburg. Those all-American family trips that are required for membership to suburbia." She smiled. "Nothing terrible ever happened to me growing up. My parents were stable and supportive. When they passed away, they left a substantial estate for Marcus and me to split. And for me to piss away on the first guy that came along, but that's a side story. My point is, I can't imagine what you went though. I can't begin to understand how broken you must feel sometimes. I'm sure losing your career in the army and everything that has happened to you since has stirred up a lot of those feelings. But I want you to know that I see beyond all that. I see the man that you want to be, that you're trying to be. You might be struggling right now, Daniel, but I do believe this will get easier for you and that you will overcome all the things that have happened to you."

He looked down and had to swallow hard. She believed in him. If he had nothing else, he had that. And he would cling to that with both hands. He just didn't know if it was enough to get through the gauntlet he was facing. The memories of his childhood were pulling at him, dragging him back to places he didn't want to ever visit again. His therapist had warned him that he was going to have to face his demons head-on if he wanted to defeat them. He was going to have to deal with the past eventually, and the sooner he did, the less damage the memories could do.

He leaned on the counter and looked up to meet her sympathetic gaze. "I wish I had your confidence, Jenna."

"You will," she said. She reached out to cup his face and nodded. "Trust me. It will be hard, but you can do this."

He covered his hand with hers and squeezed, wishing he could absorb her belief in him.

CHAPTER TWELVE

Jenna glanced over her shoulder at the fussy toddler making it nearly impossible for her parents to eat. She'd seen this very scene play out countless times since the Cantons had adopted the girl the previous year. Mira had been discontent from the day she'd been born, but her adoptive parents had the patience of saints. But even saints had their limits, and the drawn look on Kara's face as she unbuckled the strap holding Mira in the high chair spoke volumes about how close she was to hitting that limit. It was rare to see Kara without a smile on her face.

"Let me," Jenna said, closing in on them.

"Jenna, you don't have to—"

"Eat," Jenna insisted, taking Mira from the chair before Kara could.

"Thank you," Harry said as his wife fell back into the booth.

"You're welcome." She sat Mira on her hip, despite the

struggling-and-crying fit the toddler took up a notch. Bouncing as she walked away, giving the exhausted parents a bit of a break, Jenna cooed and soothed and swayed as she put a few coins into an empty container. She pressed the top on and shook it, creating enough of a distraction that Mira's crying eased. Now that she had her attention, she shook her container and continued cooing, bouncing, and soothing until the girl had forgotten she'd been throwing a fit.

Handing the toddler the container, Jenna encouraged her to shake it, smiling and laughing as she did. Thankfully the Cantons knew it was hit or miss with Mira and came in after the lunch crowd to avoid making too much of a fuss in the diner. Today was especially slow for whatever reason, so Jenna had plenty of time to entertain the baby so Kara and Harry could eat.

She was careful to keep Mira's attention in a direction away from the table where her parents were eating. Jenna had made that mistake before and the moment Mira had seen her mama across the room, not paying attention to her, all hell had broken loose. As soon as she started growing tired of the makeshift rattle, Jenna headed to a window to show her the cars going by.

Smiling, she kissed Mira's head and hugged her closer. She wasn't a bad baby. She just hadn't had an easy life and somehow seemed to know that. Kara was a midwife and had a knack for finding single mothers who needed her. Sadly, Mira's mother hadn't needed a midwife; she'd needed someone to take her unwanted baby off her hands. Jenna had to give her some credit. She'd stuck around for a good six months before telling Kara and

Harry she was going to put Mira up for adoption. They didn't hesitate to step in and take the baby in. But somehow Mira seemed to already be bitter about her birth mother's rejection.

Someone went by on a bike and Mira laughed and smacked her little hands against the window. Jenna laughed, too. Nothing lifted her spirits like hearing a baby laugh. Turning, careful not to bring Kara into Mira's line of sight, Jenna paused when she noticed Daniel sitting at the booth they tended to share for lunch. He was watching intently, but his face was neutral, making it impossible to know what he was thinking. She was getting used to his intensity, but sometimes he still shook her.

She smiled as she walked to his table. "Did you order some lunch?"

He shook his head as he slowly tore his gaze from Mira to look at Jenna. "No. I was waiting for you. Who's your friend?"

"This is little Mira and she was being a fussy-pants. We're playing until her M-O-M is done eating. This girl is a bit clingy and her you-know-who doesn't get much of a break."

His eyes softened as he smiled. "She seems to like you okay."

"Well, I'm pretty likable."

"I'd agree with that," he said.

She chuckled softly. "Did you go back to sleep after I came to work?"

"No. I got the new hinges on the kitchen cabinets though."

"Great. Maybe someday I actually will be able to rent that place."

He tensed a bit, just subtly, but before she could ask, Kara came up, calling out to Mira. The baby very nearly lurched out of Jenna's arms to get back to her mother.

"Thank you so much," Kara said to Jenna as she hugged Mira to her. "It was wonderful to actually get to eat."

"Anytime. Kara, this is Daniel. The handyman I told you about."

Kara held out her hand and Daniel shook it. "Nice to meet you. This place is looking great."

"Thank you, ma'am."

"I don't suppose you can lay roof shingles?"

"Yes, ma'am."

"Well, my husband threw a fit when I told him I was planning to fix my mother's roof by myself. Despite the fact that I'm perfectly capable, he'd rather pay someone else. Would you happen to have time in the next couple of weeks to help me get that done?"

He sat a bit taller. "Yes, ma'am."

"Great. But you have to stop calling me ma'am. You can call my mother ma'am. She'll love it."

He nodded. "Got it. I can swing by and get measurements so we can figure out what we need."

"Already done. I've ordered shingles from Carson's. They'll be in next week." She grinned at the surprise on his face. Kara loved when people underestimated her. "I just need you to tear off the old and put on the new. Do you have a number I can call when the shingles come in?"

"Just call me," Jenna offered, and ignored the lift of Kara's brows. "Kara is helping me look for some furniture for the apartment. She's the world's best bargain hunter. Undisputed."

Kara laughed. "Oh, Harry disputes plenty. I actually was going to see if you had time this evening to go look at some furniture. There was an estate sale down the street from us, and whatever didn't sell they're throwing on the curb. The furniture isn't exactly modern, but it's free. You can always throw on some couch covers or something. They'll only be there until about five today."

Jenna bit her lip. While things were slow at the moment, it wouldn't stay that way. She needed to prep for dinner and by four thirty the café was usually bustling. She had two waitresses for the evening shift, but she was usually bouncing between the floor and the kitchen.

"I can go," Daniel offered, putting an end to her debate. "I'm sure Charlie can let me use his truck a little early tonight."

She drew a breath and let it catch before saying what immediately jumped to her mind. As far as Jenna knew, Daniel hadn't seen Charlie since he'd popped into the café to warn her away from his nephew. She didn't know where Daniel sat on that whole situation and she didn't want him to confront Charlie over it. She'd only told him because she suspected he'd find out eventually and she didn't want him to feel hurt that she hadn't told him immediately. She didn't know Daniel well, but she knew enough that any loyalty and trust were important to him. She didn't want to betray that. She wanted him there, she wanted to help him, and she couldn't do that if he didn't trust her.

"That would be great, Daniel. Thank you," she said instead of warning him not to lose his temper with his uncle.

sh

As he'd done the last time he'd gone to Charlie's job site in the middle of the day, Daniel ignored the stares of the crew and headed straight for the foreman. "Charlie? Got a minute?"

Charlie looked up and the flash of fear in his eyes was unmistakable. He'd probably thought the same thing Daniel was certain Jenna had thought—there was going to be a confrontation over him dropping by the café the previous day. Daniel couldn't deny the sting, but he understood. Charlie didn't want Daniel screwing up Jenna's life the way he tended to screw up everyone else's. He got it.

Charlie nodded and put down the hammer he'd been using. He led Daniel toward a cooler set off to the side and pulled out a bottle of water. "Want one?"

"No, thanks. Jenna told me you paid her a visit."

"Danny—"

"You were right. Somebody should warn her about me." He raked his hand over his head. "I warned her, but she's convinced I can get better if somebody gives me a chance. She's even convinced me to try." He laughed softly. "I started counseling this week. This lady specializes in PTSD and all that shit. Of course she wants to dig into all the stuff with Mom and Dad, but...hell, maybe that's not a bad thing, right?"

Charlie leaned back a bit. "No, it's good. That's really good. I wish I'd known what was going on before it was too late, Danny. I would have gotten you and your mother out of there."

Daniel nodded and then exhaled. "So, um, one of Jenna's customers saw the work I'm doing at her café and asked me to help her with a project. Just replacing shingles, but it's something."

"You'll need my tools?"

He chuckled. "Wouldn't hurt. Do you mind?"

"No. I don't mind helping you. You know that, right?"

"I appreciate it. Speaking of that..." He grinned again. "Jenna wants to furnish the apartment I'm staying in. She got a lead on some estate tossing out furniture. I told her I'd go take a look. I don't suppose I can use your truck?"

Charlie took a long drink from his water. "I've had enough of this place today. Need help?"

It was Daniel's turn to lean back with surprise. "Yeah. I hadn't quite figured out how to get anything I picked up to the third floor so...help would be great."

Charlie called out to one of the guys that he was in charge for the rest of the day and headed for the trailer where his office was located. Within a few minutes, they were surrounded by awkward silence as Charlie drove them to the address Kara had given him.

"I'm proud of you," Charlie finally said. "Maybe it doesn't

seem like it given how things have unfolded the last few months, but I am."

Daniel glanced over. "I'm a homeless dishonored veteran with an attitude problem. Not much to be proud of."

"You were dealt a shitty hand and you're making the best of it. Jenna seems to be a big help."

Daniel looked out the window as they entered one of the nicer neighborhoods in the suburb he'd found himself living in. "She has been."

"She's nice."

"Yeah."

"Something going on there?"

Daniel laughed softly. "I revert back to pointing out that I'm a homeless veteran with an attitude problem. She's crazy enough to befriend me. She'd be flat-out stupid to get involved with me."

"She cares about you."

"She cares about everyone."

Charlie drew a breath. "She have anything to do with you finding a counselor?"

Daniel closed his eyes as he remembered the moment that he'd never forget—the moment Jenna's head cracked against the table because of his knee-jerk reaction to her touch. The shame he felt about that moment ran deep. "I fell asleep in one of the booths after hanging the wainscoting. She shook my leg to wake me. I grabbed her wrist and knocked her off balance."

"That knot on her head?"

"She hit the table on the way down." He swallowed hard as

his shame deepened at having to admit the truth to his uncle. "She tried to take the blame. It was her fault for surprising me. She should have known better. Mom used to pull that shit. She'd appease Dad by telling him he wouldn't have hit her if she'd just done what he'd said. I'm not my dad, Charlie. I'll never be like him. But in that moment, seeing Jenna hold an ice pack to her head, trying to take the blame for what I'd done, I saw him in me. I saw everything I hated about him in me. I wanted to leave, get as far away from her as possible so I couldn't hurt her, but she asked me to stay just until lunch so I could calm down and we could talk about it." A quiet laugh left him. "She brought iced tea, turkey, and the number for free counseling."

"And you called?"

He nodded. "I don't know if it's going to help. She thinks it will."

"It's worth a try, right?"

"Yeah. Sure."

He looked out the window as Charlie pulled into the driveway of a house. The home was as cookie-cutter as it got. A white two-story square with black shutters and hanging plants on the porch. Bushes had been trimmed into perfect squares with bright flowers evenly spaced between them.

A year ago, he never would have even dreamed of owning a home like this. He'd lived in military housing and tents since he was eighteen. But a scene flashed in his mind and seized his heart and made his breath catch. He could picture Jenna standing there, clear as day, a baby on her hip and both smiling at him as he came home from a long day at work.

He'd had a similar sensation come over him at the café when he'd walked in and seen her holding Kara's baby. She was such a natural and when she turned and smiled at him with Mira snuggled up against her, his heart had done some kind of crazy flip-flop in his chest. He'd wanted to go to them and pull them both against him and never let go. He wanted them to belong to him.

He hadn't quite understood what all that meant and hadn't been able to snap himself out of the daze until she'd walked to the table and forced him from the image forming in his mind. But now it all made sense.

He'd never considered having a family of his own, a home of his own, but somehow that suddenly felt right. Like this was where he should be—in a home like this with a wife and kid of his own. And his mind had filled that role with the only woman who ever seemed to tolerate him.

Poor Jenna.

"You coming?" Charlie asked.

Once again pulled from the thoughts of what life could be with a woman who unwittingly filled his mind, Daniel nodded. "Yeah."

"You okay?" Charlie asked after knocking on the door.

Daniel glanced around the yard. "Just reconciling my life, you know."

"Sounds deep."

He smiled when the door was opened and introduced himself and explained how they'd come to know about the furniture. The man let them in and gestured to what was left after the estate sale. "Take what you want. We were just going to put it on the curb anyway." Then he disappeared, clearly not interested.

Daniel put his hands on his hips as he looked at the teal sofa with bright pink flowers splayed in an obnoxious pattern. "Well. That's ugly."

Charlie laughed. "But it's clean and free."

"Yeah." A small table with two chairs sat behind it. More of a card or game table than a dining room table, but it was still more than what he had in the apartment. Both pieces were in near-perfect condition and Daniel imagined the owner had been elderly and particular about taking care of her furnishings. However, it was the toolbox that caught his attention. He flipped the lid back and found it full of obviously used but functioning tools. "Is this toolbox going, too?" he called out.

"It's yours," the dismissive man said.

"Nice," Charlie said. "So what are we taking?"

Daniel stood and looked at the 1980s-era couch, the highly polished table and chairs, the rusted but working toolbox, and a bookshelf with several boxes that said *kitchen* on their fronts. "All of it."

CHAPTER THIRTEEN

*J*enna walked into Daniel's apartment and had to chuckle. "Wow! Look at all this stuff." She stopped in front of the couch. "And that..."

Daniel laughed, too. "Well, as Charlie pointed out, it isn't pretty, but it was free."

"Charlie?"

The smile that spread across Daniel's face warmed her heart.

"Yeah. I went to borrow his truck and he offered to help me move the furniture, so... He got to see the place. He likes it. Oh, and he's going to bring me his guest bed and dresser. They didn't have any bedroom furniture left."

"A bed would be great, huh?"

His face sobered as he took in the apartment. "Jenna, I gotta thank you. A month ago, I didn't know what I was going to do. Now I've got an apartment—temporarily," he was quick to say.

"And a job with Kara. And my uncle... He treated me with respect today. It's been a while since he's done that."

She rubbed her hand over his arm, lightly squeezing as she said, "You deserve to be treated with respect. You're trying to move forward and get back on your feet. That's admirable. As for this apartment, it's yours for as long as you need it."

He met her gaze and there was that intensity again. His eyes had a way of drawing her in. She could get lost in his stare. He seemed to be having that same problem lately.

As she tended to do, she drew a breath and broke the gaze. "I'm sure you're hungry after moving all this furniture. Chicken and noodles."

"My second favorite," he announced.

"And look. A table."

"And chairs."

She put the bag on the table and started digging out their dinner. Usually they'd eat it at the café, but she'd been dying to see what he'd found.

"Kara seems nice," he said.

"She's very nice, but that woman is a master at bartering. She was a single mother who learned young how to convince people to trade goods instead of money. She'll get you talking and before you know it, she'll have you convinced to trade roofing her mother's house for curtains and a couch cover. Don't fall into her bargaining trap. I know her mother. She's retired, but she can afford to pay you for your work and you need the cash more than you need a couch cover."

"Thanks for the warning."

"I'm serious, Daniel. That woman is sweet as can be, but damned good at negotiating without you even realizing what you're doing. You're better off dealing with Harry if you can. He's happy to pay a bill and move on."

"They sound like complete opposites."

"Oh, they are, but it works for them." She smiled as she looked at her food. "They met in high school and then spent almost thirty years apart. As soon as they found each other again, everything just fell into place for them. They have a family now. It's romantic, really. To have someone just fit you like that. Don't you think?"

She glanced up to find that intense stare on his face again. God, he had to stop looking at her like that. She couldn't read him when he did that. She couldn't figure out what was going on inside his head, but she suspected he was judging her. Heat flushed over her cheeks and she cleared her throat. "There's that Midwestern naïveté again," she muttered.

"No. It's a nice thought. I, uh, I'd like that, too. Someone to come home to at night."

"You? You seem like such a loner."

He shrugged and turned his attention to his dinner. "I guess I always have been. I didn't see the point in getting married. The army was the most important thing in my life. I gave it my all until I didn't have enough left for a wife and kids. But...well, that's gone now and I have to think about my life without all that. It'd be nice to think that maybe...someone...could fit me like that."

She swallowed when his penetrating gaze landed on her again. For a moment, she thought he intended that *someone* to be her. For a moment, she entertained the idea herself. Daniel was nothing like Peter. Peter had been dismissive and distracted and self-centered. He'd made her feel important at first, boosting her up—buttering her up, more like. She still didn't know his true motives in having courted and married her.

She had her suspicions. She was smart, driven, and innocent enough to be a novelty for him and the ladder of people he'd had to climb to further his career. How cute it was for them to hear stories of Iowa and push her around because she was too intimidated to stand up for herself. How easily she'd been molded to be Peter's subservient little wife, supporting and pushing and planning while he left her behind.

Peter never wanted Jenna. He wanted what Jenna could do for him. He wanted a steppingstone and he'd found one in her. She'd given up her dreams to support his.

She couldn't imagine Daniel ever treating her that way. He was more protective of her than Peter had ever been. Once, at a party, a man had cornered Jenna and all but groped her until Peter walked in. Instead of defending her, Peter had dismissed the man's actions as his having had too much alcohol and Jenna being overly sensitive. She imagined if Daniel had walked in on the same, the man would have lost a few teeth before he was done with him.

She didn't condone violence, but it was nice to think there were still men out there who would defend a woman's honor. And Daniel would. That was, after all, what had gotten him in the situation he was in. Defending a woman from being attacked. Defending several women, to hear him tell the tale.

How nice it must have been to feel protected instead of used.

And when Daniel looked at her like that, she wanted nothing more than to feel like he was her protector. He was the fit she'd been looking for. He was the one who would take care of her. Look out for her. Lift her up instead of intentionally keep her down.

The notion was stupid. He was rebuilding his life, and helping her with the café just happened to be a step along his path to redemption. But every once in a while, when she least expected it, the sensation rolled through her—she wanted to be more than that.

This was one of those moments. He sat there with that look in his eyes—the one that made her wonder if maybe he felt the same draw to her. She wondered if she put her hand on his if he'd pull away or if he'd take her hand. And if he did, would it mean the same to him? She was tempted to try, but her thoughts were shattered by the sound of a knock on the door.

Daniel hesitated before leaving the table to answer. "Hey, Charlie," he said after pulling the door open.

"Sorry to just drop by. I tried to call but I guess your cell was shut off."

"Yeah. Didn't seem like something I needed at the time."

Jenna smiled when Charlie noticed her sitting at the table. "Hi, Charlie."

He nodded, seeming pleased that she'd called him by his first name this time. "Jenna. I didn't mean to interrupt your dinner."

"Have you eaten?"

"Yeah. I was just bringing that bedroom furniture by. Thought you might want it for tonight."

Jenna closed her container as she stood.

"I didn't mean to run you off," Charlie said.

"Oh, I need to get to cleaning up the café. Good to see you again," she said to Charlie as she headed out. "Night, guys."

She was unlocking the kitchen door when the men started down the stairs. She was tempted to look up at Daniel but resisted. She needed to get whatever was going on in her head worked out. Daniel had enough on his plate without her adding to it. And she certainly didn't want to scare him off. She needed him and he needed a place to stay.

He was just getting his life back on track. She wasn't going to knock him off the path he'd found himself on by throwing herself at him. Besides, he probably didn't want her like that anyway. Peter had made damned sure she knew how undesirable she was when she'd caught him with Angie. Why would he want her—a plain, boring, short Midwesterner who only bothered to wear makeup and style her hair when they were going out—when he could have someone elegant who took pride in her appearance?

Jenna glanced down at her Rolling Stones T-shirt and sighed

when she noticed mashed potatoes dried on her right breast. How long had that been there? She scratched the dried food away and felt her spirits sink. She wasn't cut out for the grace that came naturally to Angie. She'd always been a bit of a mess. She'd never cared much about her hair other than keeping it out of her face. And why wear makeup when it was just going to run anyway? Other than a swipe of mascara to distract from some of the darkness that tended to settle under her eyes, Jenna didn't see the point.

Not many men were impressed by such a lack of effort put forth by a woman. Or so Peter had said.

"Get out of my head," she breathed as she increased the tempo of her sweeping. By the time she was able to fully expel Peter's voice from her thoughts, she'd swept and mopped the floor. She was pushing the mop bucket into the kitchen when the door opened and Daniel came in with Charlie on his heels. "Did you get the bed set up?"

"Good to go," Daniel said. "I was going to show Charlie some of the bigger projects on the list. Get his input if you don't care."

"Of course not. Mind the floor. It's wet."

Their voices drifted from the dining room and a few minutes later they came back into the kitchen. Jenna finished dumping the mop bucket and putting it away before moving to where they were discussing her plumbing issues. Charlie was on the floor, looking at her pipes and clicking his tongue, when she noticed Daniel watching at her.

Charlie stood and shook his head. "I bet you've got original pipes running through this whole building."

"That's what my brother thinks, too. He said I'll probably have to replace all the plumbing sooner rather than later."

"I agree. But the good news is, you can do it in pieces. No need to tear it all out at once. It'll take longer, but you won't have to shut your doors that way."

She sighed with relief and leaned against the counter. "That'd be great."

"It's the flooring that I'm more concerned with. You don't want to do tiles," he said. "That's too damn expensive. Laminate is the way to go. There's some nice commercial grade available that will stand up to the wear and tear. I've got the measurements. I'll get some quotes, and we'll figure out what to do there."

"We?" she asked, startled.

Charlie acted as if she hadn't spoken as he focused on Daniel. "I'll get that vinyl ordered. Usually takes about two weeks to come in. We can probably get the whole lot of 'em done in a weekend. We'll take one out, reupholster it, and get it back in as soon as possible." He finally turned his attention to Jenna. "That is, if you don't mind us tackling it that way."

She shrugged. "Whatever is easiest for you guys."

"Danny gave me your budget, so no worries there. I'll find something that you can work with."

She glanced between the men. She'd missed something. Something big.

"I'll catch up with you next week sometime," he said to Daniel.

He disappeared out the kitchen door, and Daniel closed and locked it behind him.

"My head is spinning," she said once they were alone. "Is Charlie helping with the café now?"

Daniel laughed and nodded. "I didn't ask, Jen. I just showed him what I was doing and he started making plans and telling me how he can help."

"Is that okay with you?"

His smile faltered. "Is it okay with *you*? I should have asked. I'm sorry—"

"Don't be. I just want to make sure you're okay with it."

He nodded. "I was a bit concerned about your budget and how expensive some of the projects would be, but Charlie gets a contractor discount. That will save you a lot of money. You just have to reimburse him instead of buying direct from a company. And if he's willing to help with the bigger projects, they'll get done a hell of a lot faster."

"That's great. It really is, but are *you* okay with this?" She closed the distance between them and held his gaze, as if his eyes ever told her anything he was thinking. "You and Charlie seemed to have done a one-eighty today. I'm having a hard time following what's happening here."

"Well, a lot of this is his guilt, I think. And I think he feels responsible for you."

"Ah." She nodded. "Because he still thinks you might hurt me."

He focused on her forehead, pushing her hair aside, and frowned. "I told him what happened. And that I'm going to counseling. He knows I'm trying, but he also doesn't believe I'm any different than my father. I think being here and helping out is his way of looking out for you the way he couldn't look out for my mom. But this is good. He'll see that I am nothing like my father."

"You can earn his respect again."

"That's my plan. What was on your mind when we came in?" he asked quietly.

"What do you mean?"

"Your eyes were sad. Why?"

She forced a grin. "My eyes were sad?" She lowered her face when he simply stared. "Sometimes when it's quiet, I let his voice in without realizing it."

"Peter?"

She nodded.

"What was his voice saying?"

"It doesn't matter."

He put his hands to her cheeks and tilted her head back. "Tell me."

She pushed the air from her lungs. Why the hell was she finding it so hard to breathe? "It doesn't matter, Daniel."

"Tell me. Please."

The sting of tears surprised her. "After all this time, his words still hurt me sometimes. I know they shouldn't."

"What words?" His voice was a low, demanding growl this time.

As much as she loved the feel of his hands on her and his body so close, she needed to pull away so she could take a breath that didn't smell like him. Taking a few steps back, she lifted her arms out. "Look at me. I'm a mess. Food all over my shirt. My pants are getting too tight. My shoes are worn. My hair is sticking out of my bun in a million directions. No makeup. I'm a mess, Daniel. I'm always a mess. I always look like I just rolled out of bed and threw on whatever I could find because that's exactly what I do. Every morning." She ignored the tears that welled and fell from her eyes. "I get up and I come down here and I work my ass off and then I go to bed. And I...I'm never going to have what Marcus and Annie have because I...I'm a mess and Peter was right. Who the hell wants a mess like me? I'm sorry. I don't know where all this is coming from."

Daniel reached out and pulled her to him, wrapping her in his arms, and the dam broke. His hold on her was fierce, so tight the sobs welling in her chest could barely escape. The harder she cried, the harder he held her, until she felt he could crush her. But she didn't care. In fact, she wanted his arms to crush her. She wanted to crawl inside him and never have to feel like the worthless shit Peter had convinced her she was.

sh

Daniel was going to kill him. He was going to hunt down Peter Reid and bash his fucking skull in. Digging his fingers into Jenna's hair, he kissed her head and closed his eyes tight against the rage building inside him. He inhaled deeply, focusing on her scent and the feel of her body against his, forcing himself to remain calm when all he wanted to do was scream and break something—preferably her ex-husband's face.

This woman, this beautiful and amazing woman, deserved so much more than that bastard had given her. She deserved to be praised and cherished. She deserved to be honored and lifted. And that fucker had stomped on her.

He couldn't undo her past any more than she could undo his, but he was determined to help her resolve it. Just as she was helping him resolve his.

When her crying eased, he stroked his hand over her back and kissed her head one more time.

"I'm sorry," she mumbled, and sniffed.

She pulled back, and though he wasn't ready to let her go, he eased his hold on her. She put enough space between them to wipe her eyes. He grabbed some paper napkins from a stack and held them out to her. She muttered her thanks and wiped her face.

He could sense her embarrassment and cursed himself for not knowing the right thing to say to let her know that he didn't mind. In fact, he understood both the breakdown and the tears.

He wasn't big on sharing, but his counselor had let him know he wasn't going to be able to move forward until he learned to communicate. Keeping everything bottled up all the time was a disaster waiting to happen. She had suggested he find a way to talk to Jenna since she seemed to be the only good thing in Daniel's life at the moment.

He cleared his throat as he worked up the courage to push out the words that were sitting there waiting to be vocalized. "When I was a kid, I wanted to be a builder like Charlie. I didn't see him much since we lived so far away, but on the rare occasion that we did visit him, he always helped me build something. We couldn't afford a Big Wheel—remember those?"

Her voice was hoarse when she answered, "Yeah."

"Charlie helped me put wheels on a board and we painted it. The other kids had three-wheelers, but I had this really cool homemade skateboard. Rode that thing till it broke. When it did, I tried to build another one. My dad caught me and asked what I thought I was doing. I told him I was going to grow up to be like Uncle Charlie. Man, that set him off. I was eight, maybe nine at the time. He stood over me the whole time telling me how stupid I was. When I couldn't get the wheels on right, I decided he was right. I was too stupid, so I gave up. I threw it all away because my dad convinced me I wasn't good enough. People like that, like my dad and your ex, they have a way of finding ways to break everyone around them. I was good enough to make that skateboard. And you're good enough to own this café. And you deserve what your brother has. And any man who can't see how beautiful you are without fancy clothes and makeup doesn't deserve you anyway."

She sniffed and wiped her nose before offering him a soft smile. "Thank you." She hesitated and then walked into his arms again, this time with an embrace of her own instead of collapsing against him under the weight of his hold on her.

He hugged her back, and the need to kiss her hit him. Not like the comforting kiss to her head like before, but a kiss to let her know he meant what he said. He'd have been so honored to have a woman like her. To deserve someone like her.

For a moment, he recalled standing in the driveway of that house and seeing her standing there holding a baby on her hip, waiting for him to join them. Just like before, the sense of contentment that washed over him was something he'd never expected to feel.

"Jenna," he said, once again preparing to let his words fly instead of forcing them down.

"What the hell is going on?" A voice boomed from the swinging doors.

Daniel instinctively turned, putting himself between Jenna and the intruder. Her brother stormed toward him, his eyes full of fury as he looked from his sister to the man in front of her.

"What did you do to her?"

"Nothing," Jenna insisted. Then she moved between Daniel and Marcus. "I had a bad night. He was letting me vent."

Marcus seemed to be weighing whether he should believe her before he focused on Daniel again. "Is this your new *handyman?*"

Jenna sighed and Daniel stiffened. "What are you doing here so late, Marcus?"

"We were expecting you at game night. When you didn't show and we couldn't get you on the phone, we got worried."

Jenna moaned and turned to the petite blonde beside her brother. "Annie, I'm so sorry. I completely spaced out."

"Are you okay?" she said, but her voice was a bit hard to understand. Jenna had told him she'd been hurt. This must have been a side effect of her injury.

"I'm fine. I just forgot about tonight."

Daniel looked at Marcus to find the man giving him a hard stare.

He held his hand out, hoping to smooth things over a bit. "Daniel Maguire."

"Marcus Callison." His handshake was firmer than necessary. A silent way of asserting dominance.

"Were you crying?" Annie asked.

"I had a bad day. I was venting to Daniel and just... I forgot I was supposed to come over when the café closed. I'm sorry."

Annie looked at him. "Daniel?"

"Yes. He's...he's my handyman."

Annie smirked and her eyes twinkled with what Daniel could only suspect was a bit of mischief. He wanted to laugh, but Marcus was still standing, staring him down.

"Marcus," Annie chastised, and then looked at Jenna. "He's been out of sorts since you hired someone."

Marcus sighed and turned to his sister. "We don't know anything about you."

"I know plenty," Jenna stated quietly but harshly. "Don't be rude."

Daniel usually would have smarted off. Said something challenging. Asserted his own dominance. But Marcus was Jenna's brother and he meant the world to her. If there were any chance at all that he'd have Jenna in his life for the long term, even just as a friend, he'd have to become friends with Marcus as well. He leaned against the counter and rested his hands on the counter beside either of his hips instead of crossing them in the challenge that he wanted to present. He shrugged and did his best to appear relaxed as he asked, "What do you want to know?"

"Are you licensed to do this kind of work in Iowa?"

"Yes."

"What kind of experience do you have?"

"Twenty-five years in the army building shelters in war-torn countries."

Marcus nodded. "So you're originally from Iowa?"

"No. I grew up in Jersey but my uncle lives here. He has a construction company. Offered me a job when I got out of the army. And before you ask, I left because I lost my temper with one of his crew. I didn't want to put him in a bad position."

"Why'd you lose your temper?"

"The guy was bragging about beating on his wife. Didn't sit well with me."

Marcus drew a breath. "I can respect that. You're aware of Jenna's budget?"

"Yes, sir."

"And you know about the plumbing issues?"

Daniel nodded. "Had my uncle in earlier this evening to give me a second opinion."

"And what'd you decide?"

"We're going to replace all the plumbing in sections so Jen doesn't have to close."

Marcus seemed pleased. "And the electrical?"

"I've already rewired the bad outlet by the coffeepots. But I'm not concerned enough to move the electrical to the top of the list. Jen wants the dining room updated first. Then I'll hit the plumbing and electrical simultaneously while we have the walls torn apart."

"Happy?" Jenna asked harshly, putting herself between Marcus and Daniel.

"I'm just looking out for you."

"I know, but I'm not a complete idiot, Marcus. I can hire a goddamn handyman without you looking over my shoulder."

Marcus softened his posture. "What happened today that had you so upset?"

Jenna sagged a bit and Daniel had to clench his hands into fists to stop from reaching out to comfort her again. "Doesn't matter."

"Well," Annie said decisively, "now that we know Jen is safe and sound, we should go. Marcus," she said more firmly when he didn't move, "we should go. *Now*." She smiled at Daniel. "It was nice meeting you." She spoke more slowly when she addressed him, as if to make sure he could understand her.

He smiled. "You, too, ma'am. Jenna talks about you a lot."

"Oh, good things I hope."

"So far so good."

"Come on," she hissed, pulling at her husband. "Night, guys. We'll lock up."

"What's the hurry?" Marcus asked as she shoved him through the swinging doors.

Jenna faced Daniel when they were gone. "Thank you for keeping your cool. I know it wasn't easy."

He tried to fight it, but couldn't help but grin. "You saw that struggle, huh?"

"I did. And I don't blame you. He came across a bit strong."

"I don't blame him. He should be protective of you."

"Well, he is." She glanced at the door before meeting his gaze. "So, um, I made salsa to take to game night at Annie and Marcus's, but I think I'd rather just hang out and watch a movie or something. Want to join me?"

What he wanted was to pull her into another embrace and never let her out of his arms again. "I never pass on salsa."

Musical laughter left her, an amazing contradiction to the sobbing sounds she'd released earlier. A bit of pride touched him, knowing he'd been the cause of that laugh. He opened the kitchen door and let her lead the way.

CHAPTER FOURTEEN

*J*enna was surprised she'd made it all the way to lunchtime before Annie and Marcus slid into a booth at the diner. Annie smiled and Jenna knew she was in for an inquisition. And she had no doubt it was about Daniel. Unlike Marcus with his questions about experience and licensure, Annie was going to ask the tough questions. Like how was it that there was such a handsome man in Jenna's kitchen and she hadn't told her sister-in-law yet?

Jenna sat, wishing she could use the crowd as an excuse, but the rainy day had thinned out the usual Saturday gathering. "I'm sorry about last night. I really did just forget."

"Better day today?" Marcus asked.

"Much."

"You're working too many hours. You should start closing one day a week."

Jenna and Marcus had this conversation at least twice a

week. She would love to close an entire day, but she had to settle for opening late and closing early on Sunday. The after-church lunch crowd was just too good to turn away, and she had regulars Monday through Friday. And Saturday was usually a steady flow of people. She needed the income more than she needed the time off. She frowned at her sister-in-law. "Can you make him stop? Please."

"Go away, Marcus," Annie insisted.

He lifted his brows at her.

"We need girl time."

"Oh, no," Jenna moaned. She looked at Marcus. "Can you make *her* stop?"

His confusion slowly faded to disapproval. "You're not dating the handyman, are you?"

"*No.*"

"Then what do you need to discuss that I can't overhear?"

"*Why* she isn't dating the handyman. Go."

Jenna frowned as she stood and let her brother out. Then she plopped back down. "Are you and Marcus aware that I'm an adult?"

"We are," Annie said. "And we're so proud of the woman you've become."

Jenna sneered at her sarcasm.

"Daniel's cute."

Like she needed Annie to point that out. The first time she'd seen him without his scruffy beard and hair, she'd nearly swooned. "Hmm."

"Looks like he gives good hugs."

"Oh, Annie. Get to the point."

"He likes you."

"Well, I'd like to think we've become friends."

"Maybe more?"

Jenna shook her head. "I have to work with the man. I don't need these thoughts in my head."

"Oh, because you haven't thought them already?"

She stared at Annie for a good twenty seconds before she chuckled. "Fine. Maybe a little."

"How much is a little?"

"Not enough to make a fool of myself by acting on them. I'm sorry I made you worry last night. It won't happen again."

"Don't dismiss me," Annie warned, "or I'll have to ask Daniel why he isn't courting you yet."

"You wouldn't."

She pointed to her head. "I have brain damage."

"And you can't always control your impulses," Jenna finished. "How long are you going to use that excuse?"

"Forever." She smiled innocently, but if she'd had horns, Jenna was certain they'd be shining brightly. "Come on, Jen. There was a handsome man standing in your kitchen at ten o'clock at night with his big, strong arms wrapped around you and you don't feel that's worth talking to your sister about?"

She hated when Annie played the sister card. They'd both grown up with only brothers, and while Annie now had two sisters-in-law via her brothers, Annie was the only "sister" Jenna would ever have. "*Fine*. Daniel is a great guy. He's really nice, but he's been struggling lately and he's trying to get back on his feet. The last thing he needs is me getting in his way."

Annie's smile faltered. "Why would you be in his way?" Several tense moments passed before she nodded. "Oh. The Ghost of Husband Past strikes again."

Taking a deep breath, Jenna lifted her shoulders and let them fall as she pushed her breath out. "I don't want Peter in my head, but he's there and he kicks my feet out from under me when I least expect it. I'd been doing really well, you know. Ever since Daniel started working on the café I've started feeling like I could really succeed at this."

"Because you can."

"Yeah. And then I started thinking how nice it would be if the café were successful enough that I could finally have a life outside of this building. Hire a few more people, have some time off...maybe even meet someone. And then there he was, reminding me how much of a loser I am. Daniel saw in my eyes that I was beating myself up and pushed to find out why. And"— she waved her hand in front of her face—"emotional vomit just spewed out of me and there I was sobbing and the poor man had to try to comfort me. It was humiliating."

"He didn't look put out, Jen. He looked worried. And he looked like he couldn't wait for Marcus and me to leave so he could be alone with you."

"He couldn't wait for Marcus to leave and take his evil glare with him."

"Your brother worries about you."

"I know. I wish he wouldn't."

"It took me an hour to convince him you were perfectly safe with Daniel. You are safe with him, right?"

Jenna looked out the window, but she was seeing the way Daniel looked at her. He didn't even try to hide it anymore. He'd used to turn away when she'd catch him staring. Now he just locked his gaze on hers and she was the one who had to fight to break away. Part of her didn't want to; part of her wanted to stare him down—but if he could overpower her with his eyes, he could break her with his touch.

She was already broken.

"Jenna?" Annie asked, disrupting her thoughts. "Is there something I need to know about Daniel?"

She swallowed. "He's...intense. I don't mean that in a bad way. He doesn't scare me or anything like that. In fact, I don't think I've ever felt safer than when I'm with him. He's so concerned about my safety. He's concerned about me being in the café alone so much. He's been teaching me some self-defense. He's scheduled estimates with a few security companies and put new locks on all the windows. He tries to be subtle about it, but every night he stands outside to make sure I get to my door okay. He's probably about as protective as Marcus," she said with a light laugh.

"Those are all good signs," Annie said. "Why do you look worried?"

"Because sometimes I think... The way he looks at me

maybe…" She sighed heavily, frustrated at her inability to finish a sentence. "Look, I don't think I should be dating or even thinking about it. Not when Peter's memory can still get to me so easily. That's just setting a new relationship up for failure."

"Honey, the best way to stop letting that man get to you is to replace his voice with someone else's. His negativity will drown out everything else if you don't let some positivity inside your head. I have no idea if Daniel is the one, but if I had to judge by just the few minutes that I saw him with you last night, I'd guess that he'd like to try."

"It's not just that. Annie, you know me. I don't have your strength. I'm a follower. I'm submissive. Daniel spent most of his life in the army. He's strong and…overwhelming. He could swallow me whole. Just like Peter did. But he's much stronger than Peter. Peter was charming and manipulative. Daniel is just…"

"Intense."

"Yes."

"First of all, you're stronger than you give yourself credit for. You just haven't learned how to exert that strength. Secondly, it's okay to let someone else have control sometimes. You just have to make sure that the person who has control also has your best interests in mind. Peter never did. I don't know Daniel, so I can't speak to his motives, but you're a smart woman and you learned a lot from your divorce. I think you'd recognize the signs a lot sooner now than you did when you were inexperienced in the world of devious men. Don't you?"

Jenna sighed. "Yeah. I guess."

"You've looked happier lately, Jen. Less burdened. It's been a nice change."

"Just because Daniel wants to fix up the café doesn't mean he wants to fix me, too."

"Trust your instinct. If Daniel isn't the one, then he isn't the one. But you'll never know if you're too scared to even consider it."

She again imagined him looking at her. Felt his arms around her. No one had ever made her feel so protected, so cherished. She didn't know if that was his intent, but it certainly was the effect. "Maybe I'll consider it."

"Good. Now I'm going to wave your brother over here and when he asks what's going on, I'm going to tell him I just talked you out of running off to Vegas to marry the handyman."

"Oh, Annie. He'll freak."

She smiled. "I know. It'll be fantastic."

Daniel ground his teeth together as he stared at the ceiling. He was so damned frustrated with himself. After crawling into bed last night...and being incredibly happy to do so...he'd replayed the scene in the kitchen over and over in his mind. The heartbreak on Jenna's face had nearly killed him. The need to protect her had overwhelmed him. And then the need to prove to her that she was worthy consumed him.

He had spent half the night trying to think of ways to show her that she was deserving of all the things she felt she wasn't. That she didn't have to dress fancily or wear makeup to be beautiful. He'd seen how beautiful she was the first time he'd watched her dump dirty mop water into the alley. He'd been taken with her from the moment he saw her. He hated that anyone would make her feel less than what she was.

He also hated that every single idea he'd had to make her feel good about herself involved money. He couldn't buy her flowers. He couldn't take her to dinner. He couldn't treat her to an evening out. He couldn't even take her for ice cream. He had *maybe* fifteen dollars left to his name. The only thing that proved was that *he* wasn't worthy of *her*.

Yesterday he'd been feeling pretty damned good about himself. He'd made huge inroads with Charlie and he actually had a bed to sleep in and a couch to sit on. He had big plans for Jenna's café. He'd held Jenna in his arms and soothed her broken heart. He'd finally been able to give something back to her, even if it was as simple as a little comfort. But comfort wasn't going to make her life easier. Comfort wasn't going to stretch her budget so she could have some downtime.

A short scream followed by what sounded like a scuffle on the stairs yanked Daniel from his thoughts. He was on his feet and jerking the door open just as Jenna reached his landing.

Putting his hands to her face, he scanned the area. "What happened?"

She looked at him with wide eyes. "Uh, I...uh..."

"Jenna. What happened?"

"Nothing. I was...running. The sky just opened up." She blinked a few times.

He looked up, noticing the downpour for the first time. He'd been too focused on getting to her to realize it was raining outside and she was drenched.

"So you're okay?"

"Yeah. I'm fine. Um..." She diverted her eyes, rolling them toward the ceiling. "I brought lunch."

He grabbed the bag of food she was holding and stepped aside. "Come in."

"I failed miserably in my attempt to hurry so I didn't get soaked," she said, not moving. "I should go put on dry clothes."

He set the bag on the table and started to tell her there was no point in going back out when it was still raining, but the words lodged in his throat at the expression on her face. He didn't have a huge amount of experience with women, but he was pretty certain there was a longing in her eyes as she skimmed her gaze over him before looking away.

He tightened his hand to make the fist that usually helped him fight temptation when she was around. It didn't help. In fact, the blush on her cheeks made his desire for her flare. Much like the first time he'd seen her in the kitchen of the café, she was soaking wet. Strands of dark hair stuck to her face. Her shirt, with *Benatar* spelled out in shades of purple and fuchsia, clung to her. He lowered his gaze; he couldn't stop himself. She took a breath, and he swallowed hard as he watched her breasts press against the thin gray material.

His mind was screaming for him to stay back, keep some space between them, but his body ignored the command and in just a few short strides, he was standing a breath away from her. She resembled a deer in headlights, frozen in fear.

Damn it. He'd scared her again.

"You're right," he said, his voice coming out in a growl he didn't intend. "You should go put on dry clothes."

"You should...put on clothes," she whispered.

He looked down at himself. *Oh.* No wonder she looked terrified. He was standing in front of her in nothing but a pair of tight boxer briefs that did nothing to hide his reaction to being so close he could smell her. It'd been a long time since he'd had a woman. And even longer since he'd felt so damned attracted to one. He closed his eyes and tried to grab hold of an image to tame his body's response to her, but before he could settle on something sufficiently disturbing, she lightly ran her fingers over the right side of his chest, just below his collarbone. He jerked his eyes open as the heat from her fingertips shot straight to his erection. She pulled her hand back but he caught it before she could lower it.

"Sorry." She stared at where she'd been touching. "Your scars..."

He hesitated before putting her hand back to the splattering of raised flesh that stretched down to his hip. She traced the bumps as if to memorize each one as she moved her fingers. The old wound seemed to heal as she went. Somehow the skin didn't feel so tight.

"What happened?" she asked, finally focusing on his eyes again. Her breath smelled sweet. Like the tea she sipped most of the day. He imagined her lips would taste of the drink—sugar and a hint of the lemon she always squeezed before stirring with her straw and adding extra ice. He didn't realize he was staring at her mouth until she pulled her bottom lip between her teeth in the way that she did when she was nervous.

"We were repairing a school when we were attacked. Not everyone wants things to get better over there. I got lucky. My wounds are only skin-deep. A lot of people died that day."

That look settled on her face again. Not pity; she wasn't feeling sorry for him. She looked like another piece of his puzzle had fallen into place. She was figuring him out. Learning to see through his tough exterior. She lowered her hand and he instantly missed her touch, but the fire in her eyes was more than enough to make him feel her heat.

In that moment, he realized it wasn't fear he'd been seeing in her eyes; it was uncertainty. Probably the same trepidation he'd been feeling. There was an undeniable magnetism between them that seemed to be constantly increasing.

He'd known it much longer than she had. He'd felt it the first time he'd seen her. She seemed to be realizing it now as well, but her lack of confidence was making her question what was happening between them. He wouldn't stand for that.

"Do my scars bother you?"

"No."

"Does my past scare you?"

"No."

"Do *I* scare you?"

"*No.*"

He swallowed hard. "Do you want to know what I was thinking about when I heard you on the stairs?"

She nodded.

He brushed a strand of hair from her face. "I was thinking how much I want to do something to show you that your ex was wrong. You are amazing, Jenna. I want to buy you flowers, take you to dinner, but..." Shame punched him in the gut. "I can't. I *literally* can't. I don't have a thing to offer you, and you deserve everything."

She shook her head slowly. "I don't need those things. They're just things. Look what you've done for me. Look at this apartment. Look at the café."

"I can't take care of you."

"You already are."

He put his hands on her face, forcing her to see how serious he was. "I won't be my father. I won't take and take and never give back."

"You *do* give back, Daniel."

"Not in the way that matters. But I'm working on it. This job with Kara will lead to more jobs. And I'll get back on my feet. *Then* I'll deserve you." He brushed his thumb over her lips. "And *then* I'll claim you as mine."

Curiosity mixed with the lust in her eyes. "Claim me?"

He touched her full lips again. "Once I kiss you, you'll be mine." He pushed the damp strands of hair from her face. "Mine to keep, to protect, to provide for. To keep satisfied."

She lifted her chin and he thought she was trying to look offended. She failed. Her eyes betrayed her. She liked the idea. "That's archaic."

"Which part?"

"All of it."

"No. It's a show of my respect for you. Until I can give you a better life, you're better off without me."

"But…what if… What if I want you to claim me now?"

"I won't."

"Well. What if *I* claim *you?*"

Running her thumb over his lips as he'd done to her, she stared into his eyes. There was that familiar shadow of doubt behind her determination. She always seemed to be fighting for her confidence. She wouldn't if she could see herself through his eyes.

"What if I make you mine?" she asked, distracting him from his thoughts. "To protect and keep and…satisfy?"

He swallowed hard. He wasn't expecting her to turn the tables on him. "I'm the man."

"That's sexist."

"*Archaic*," he said.

He pulled her freezing-cold wet clothes against his warm flesh. He wrapped one arm around her waist and dug the fingers of his other hand in her hair, tilting her head back so he could look down into her eyes. She gripped his hips, pressing her fingertips into his sides, and pulled him even closer.

Damn it, she was testing every ounce of his resolve.

"I *need* to take care of you. Do you understand that?"

"Yes. But—"

"No, buts." He pressed his lips to her forehead.

"Kissing my head isn't claiming me?"

He smirked. "Oh, you'll know when I stake my claim." He pressed his erection against her and she gasped. "Go put on dry clothes. I need to go take care of my…problem." He smiled when her eyes widened and her cheeks blushed.

"Daniel," she called as he headed for the door.

He turned, but her back was still to him.

"What about lunch?"

Shit, he didn't even want to leave. "Better eat without me. This could take a while." He grabbed her lunch from the table and held it out to her. "I'll see you for dinner, though."

CHAPTER FIFTEEN

*J*enna couldn't stop thinking about those few
moments that had passed between her and
Daniel in his apartment. Damn it, she should
have just tackled him and "staked her claim" like she'd wanted to.
Damn his pride. He'd left her fluttering and burning and off
balance.

She hadn't been able to focus on anything since coming back
down to the café. She'd mixed up orders, forgotten names, and
refilled the wrong drinks more times in one afternoon than in
the three years of owning the café. Her mind was on Daniel—or
more specifically, his promise to claim her.

"Ma'am," someone barked, snapping her out of her fog. "I've
asked for ketchup twice."

"Right. Sorry." She scurried to the kitchen, grabbed a bottle,
and rushed back. "I'm so sorry, sir."

He gestured around the near-empty dining room. "It's not

like you're swamped. If you can't handle waiting a few tables, maybe you should..."

She waited for him to finish, but he was distracted by something behind her. She turned. Daniel stood a few feet away, his posture defensive, daring the man to finish.

"Is everything else okay?" she asked her customer.

"Fine," he muttered.

She crossed the dining room. "Don't glare at my customers."

"He's being rude."

"I forgot his ketchup twice."

"That's not reason enough to be an ass."

"Stop it," she warned when he looked toward the table again. "It's your fault anyway."

He creased his brow at her. "What'd I do?"

She gently pushed him onto a stool and smirked. "I think you know."

He grinned, and she wanted to brush her fingers over his lips again.

"Hungry?"

"You have no idea."

She laughed softly and shook her head. "I have baked chicken."

"How about just some onion rings?"

"Coming right up." She headed into the kitchen and dumped an order into the basket before easing it into the fryer. She set the timer and pulled out a plate and then went back to the dining room to fill a glass for him. "Soda?"

He smiled slightly, as if he were thinking about something else. "How about some of that tea you like so much?"

She hesitated. Why did asking for tea seem like he was conspiring? She filled a glass and dropped a lemon in before setting it in front of him. "Why do you look guilty of something?"

He shrugged. "Don't I always?"

She chuckled and then glanced to the table where the disgruntled ketchup man was sitting. His glass was empty so she walked around to offer him a refill.

"Is the service always this bad here?" he asked.

She wanted to point out that she'd been at his table less than five minutes ago, but instead just smiled. "Diet, right?"

"That's right."

She bit her tongue as she headed for the drink dispenser. This wasn't the first time she'd dealt with someone like this, but the fire in Daniel's eyes as she headed in his direction let her know she should be more concerned about him than her customer's dissatisfaction.

"Relax," she whispered as she passed him. She filled the drink, set it on the man's table with a smile, and went back to the kitchen to get Daniel's onion rings. She slid the plate and a bottle of ketchup on the counter and left to tend to the handful of customers in the café. She refilled a few coffee cups, amazed at how she was suddenly able to function again now that Daniel was there, and made her way back to her disgruntled customer.

"Can I get you anything else?" she asked happily, despite the scowl on his face.

"No, thanks."

She set the coffeepot on an empty table next to his and pulled her order pad from her apron.

"You're seriously going to make me pay for this shitty meal?"

She ripped his bill from the book. "You can tip as you see fit, but you will pay for the food you ate."

He grabbed her wrist as she laid the paper on the table. Her newfound instinct kicked in and she turned and yanked free in the way Daniel had trained her. As she did, she noticed her teacher practically launching from his seat.

"No!" She put her hands up to stop him. Pressing them against Daniel's chest, she dug her heels in. "No. No."

He tore his fiery gaze from the man to look at her.

"No," she said more gently.

Returning his hard stare to the man, he said through clenched teeth, "Pay your bill and leave."

The threat in his words made her quake inside, and he wasn't even talking to her. She didn't pay attention to the man, but assumed he was doing as told, because she was certain that if he dared to defy the order, Daniel would push her aside and break the man's neck. Something slapped against the tabletop—money most likely—and then the sound of leg chairs scraping over the floor filled the eerily quiet diner and brought her a sense of relief. The man was leaving.

But then glass shattered, and she turned. He'd knocked the half-filled coffeepot from the table on his way out. She felt the rumble in Daniel's chest just moments before a primal sound left him, giving her the distinct impression that he was out for blood and probably wouldn't stop until the man who was stomping toward the door delivered.

Not too long ago, Jenna had been thinking how nice it would be to have a man protect her rather than throw her to the wolves as Peter had done, but the reality was vastly different than what she'd imagined. Fear gripped her—not for herself, but that Daniel could really hurt that man and get himself in trouble.

Then what? How would he get on his feet if he were in jail? He wouldn't, and that would be all the evidence he'd need that he wasn't good enough for her. And then he'd leave her. And she couldn't let that happen. She *wouldn't* let that happen.

Daniel gripped her upper arms and moved her aside, but she fisted his shirt and pulled, refusing to let him go out the door that the man slammed on his way out. "Don't." She tugged harder on Daniel's shirt. "Just let him go."

Backing down, doing nothing, wasn't in his nature and she knew it. He took a step, bumping into her, but she bumped back.

"Let him go. Daniel. Let him go."

He exhaled loudly, and finally eased his stance. Pulling her hands from his shirt, he lifted her hand, examining he wrist. "Did he hurt you?"

"No. I'm okay." She put her fingers to his face, drawing his attention away from her arm and offering him a smile. "Did you see that? I *kung fu*-ed my way right outta that bastard's grip."

He didn't smile.

"Daniel. I'm fine."

"I was sitting right there. He shouldn't have had a chance to touch you."

She sighed. "Really? Not even a pat on the back for defending myself?"

One of her regular customers called out her name. She hadn't even noticed Paul O'Connell standing beside Daniel. His had been the last mug refilled by the doomed coffeepot. And he also happened to be Annie's younger brother. There was no hope of keeping Marcus from hearing about this. But at least he'd hear how Daniel rushed to her defense. That would score him a few points with her brother.

Paul's wife, Dianna, rushed around him and took Jenna's hand, as Daniel had done. "Did he hurt you?"

"No. I'm fine." She stepped back and offered a smile. "I'm fine, everyone. I'm so sorry for the disturbance. There's always one, right?" she said as lightly as she could. "Go finish your lunch," she told the O'Connells. They both hesitated to return to their table, but when they did she turned to Daniel. "Thank you."

"He never should have had the chance to touch you."

"This is exactly why you're teaching me to defend myself, right? And I did. Now sit. Finish your onion rings. I need to clean this mess up."

"I'll clean it up."

"Your snack will get cold."

"I don't care. Check on your customers."

Before she could argue, he went to the back. She started another pot of coffee and walked to each table, reassuring her customers one by one that she was fine and again apologizing for the scene.

sh

Daniel's conviction to teach Jenna self-defense had relaxed a bit after she'd learned a few basic moves. Seeing her use what he'd taught her should have eased his mind, but his determination to make sure she could keep herself safe grew. Seeing that man grab her had lit Daniel on fire. The rage burned so hot and so fast, he was surprised flames weren't shooting out of his eyes by the time Jenna stopped him.

And good thing she did. He was eager to snap that bastard's wrist in half for daring to put his hand on Jenna.

Splashing water on his face in the café sink, he tried to extinguish the burning anger that still roiled inside his chest. He'd spent the rest of the afternoon on that stool, watching, keeping an eye on things in case the man returned. She'd accused him of standing guard. He was. He'd been on high alert until she clicked off the open sign and locked the front door.

Even then he wasn't ready to leave her alone. He helped her

clean, his muscles tense and nerves fully aware and ready to respond on cue.

"All done," she announced after putting the last of the ham she'd been cutting into the fridge. Tomorrow's special was a meat-lover's omelet. She'd spent an hour preparing ham, bacon, and sausage to make her morning a bit easier. Taking her apron off, she hung it on a hook and walked to the sink where she washed her hands and accepted the towel he held out to her. "You look tired."

He rolled his shoulders. "I'm good."

"You've been hyperaware ever since that man left this afternoon. He won't be back."

"You don't know that."

"I deal with disgruntled customers on a regular basis. Some people think if they start complaining early enough in the meal, it justifies not leaving a tip."

"People grab you like that all the time?"

"No. That was new. But I handled it. Thanks to your brilliant training skills."

He smiled when she did. He couldn't help it. Her smile eased the stress in his chest. Sliding his arm around her waist, he pulled her closer. "I would have killed him if he'd hurt you."

"I think everyone there realized that."

"I won't apologize for that. But I am sorry if I frightened anyone."

"You didn't. They were all very glad you were there to stand up for me."

He put his forehead to hers and closed his eyes. "I don't think you know what you're getting into with me, Jen. You should tell me to leave."

Instead, she whispered, "Stay." She tilted her face, brushing her lips over his, but he turned enough to stop her from being able to fully kiss his mouth. Her lips fell on his cheek.

He dug his fingertips into her sides. "You're asking for trouble."

"And you're killing me."

He caught her hand as she trailed her fingertips over his cheek. If she didn't stop touching him like that, he wasn't going to be able to resist her. "You're not making it easy for me to be honorable."

"Good."

He turned his face into her palm. Her skin was slightly rough against his lips, dry from washing so many times throughout the day. He didn't mind. He didn't mind at all. In fact, he couldn't wait to feel her hands on his body again, touching more than just his scars.

He pulled her hand from his face, entwining their fingers as he did. "Come on."

He led her from the café and upstairs, stopping at her apartment door. He put a kiss on her head after she unlocked her door. He waited until she engaged the locks before heading upstairs. Inside his apartment, now filled with secondhand furniture, he sat at the table and grabbed the pad of paper he'd been making notes on before venturing down to the café earlier in the day.

He was a long way from making Maguire Construction a reality, but he had plans on paper. That was a hell of a lot closer than he'd been the day before, and he knew that with Jenna believing in him, he'd be even closer tomorrow.

CHAPTER SIXTEEN

*J*enna wouldn't exactly say she was disgruntled, but damn that Kara Canton for giving Daniel something to do *outside* the café. Actually, she was thrilled for Daniel. He'd come into the café the night before dirty, exhausted, and happier than she'd ever seen him. He'd laughed as he ate his meatloaf and told her how Kara had indeed tried to barter for his work. Kara's mother had saved him by offering a fee and asking if he wanted cash or a check, provoking from Kara what Daniel said was the biggest eye roll he'd ever seen from a grown woman.

Today was day two of working on the roofing project. Day two of not being able to run up to Daniel's apartment with lunch and sit across the table from him and hear his stories while enduring his powerful stare. She'd come to understand that stare much better in the last few days. His intensity, his dark looks, and his looming physique might have been threatening to others, but were pure comfort for her. He used his natural intimidation to keep others at bay, but it'd drawn her in and she could hardly stand that he'd been so far away the last two days.

But having a bit of distance between them was good, too. Not only because Daniel was finally working for pay, which was so important to him, but because she was doing exactly what she'd told Annie she would do. Daniel's dominant personality was swallowing her. She could hardly function without him near.

The other day, all the fumbling and mistakes that had gotten her customer so frustrated that he'd grabbed her was evidence of how dependent she was becoming on Daniel. She swore she'd never let herself get that tied to another man after Peter, but here she was, walking into another web of co-dependency.

Annie was right—Peter had taken advantage of her and Daniel never would. Daniel would swallow her up and protect her, but even so, Jenna had to stop being so reliant on everyone around her. She'd gone from needing her parents to needing Peter to needing Marcus to needing Daniel. That cycle had to end and having Daniel out of the café was a good start.

But damned if her heart didn't soar like a freaking beach kite at the sight of Charlie's truck pulling into a parking spot in front of the café. She tamped her excitement down when she noticed Charlie wasn't just dropping Daniel off, but was following him in. She grabbed two menus as they sat at the counter.

Charlie waved it off. "Can't stay. Just wanted to talk over some options on the flooring."

She listened to his suggestions, looked at the samples, and studied the quote. Damn. Any way he put it, she was going to end up spending more money than she wanted. Part of her desperately wanted to wait to talk to Marcus. He knew her budget in and out. Part of her wanted to look at Daniel and have him tell her what to do. But she took a breath and pointed to the second-cheapest option—the one Charlie said would cost a bit more but would last much longer. "That one. Let's do that."

Charlie smiled. "Good choice. Danny, let's measure one more time so I don't over-order."

She tried to quell her nerves as they did their best to stay out of the way while determining how much flooring to order. She'd already made it clear to only replace the floor in the dining room. She'd suffer with cracked linoleum in the kitchen for a while longer. With the measurements complete, Charlie let her know he'd get that taken care of and that her vinyl was on the way—he and "Danny" had already planned to get the booths tackled the following week. By then, the flooring should have been in and ready for installation.

She thanked him, handed him a to-go cup of sweet tea, and watched him leave before looking at Daniel. "Oh. My. God. Did I really just approve your uncle to spend that much money?"

Daniel put his arm around her shoulder and led her to the counter. "You did. And it will be worth it."

Sitting on the stool next to him, she exhaled her anxiety. "Did you finish the roofing project?"

"Yup. And guess what?"

"Hmm?"

"The lady across the street asked if I knew anyone who could build raised gardens for her. She's finding it too difficult to get up and down these days and wants them done as soon as possible so they are ready for planting in the spring."

Jenna lifted her brows. "And whom did you suggest?"

"Some guy I know."

She laughed lightly. "I'm so happy for you."

"And I'm happy for you. You took the plunge on two of the biggest projects yet. I know letting go of that money is frightening, but believe me"—he ran his hand reassuringly over her arm—"it's going to be worth it."

How could she not believe him when his eyes held so much promise? Everything was coming together. Everything was falling into place.

How incredibly terrifying was that?

He opened the toolbox that he'd set on the floor next to his chair and pulled out a bag. "I got paid for the roofing job today. I got you something."

He didn't have to do that, but she didn't want to discard his effort by saying so. He already appeared uncertain as he held the bag out to her. She smiled as she accepted his present. "Thank you."

"Open it before you thank me. I'm not sure you'll like it."

She reached into the plain white bag and pulled out a T-shirt, laughing as the words *Hold Me Closer* above a picture of Tony Danza unfolded before her.

He sat taller at her reaction. "You like it? It isn't exactly an Elton John vintage tee, but it was as close as I could get."

"I love it. It's great." She touched his hand. "I will wear it with pride." And she would, mostly because he'd bought it for her.

"I hope so."

"Tell me what you want for dinner and then go get a shower. I'll bring it up to you."

"Have you eaten yet?"

She shook her head, and he smiled.

"Good. Bring enough of whatever you want for two. I want to hear about your day."

Another string of that emotional attachment she was trying to avoid attached itself to her heart. "I want to hear about yours, too."

sh

Daniel was bone-tired as he dragged himself from the shower. He really just wanted to fall into bed and sleep, but Jenna was coming with dinner and that was worth staying awake. He pulled on clean clothes and was clearing off the table when she knocked on his door. Despite his weariness, his heart felt light. He opened the door and gestured for her to come in.

Last time she'd been in his apartment, the attraction between them had nearly consumed him. He'd admitted his intentions with her and she'd questioned why he had to wait. She wanted him, too. She wanted to be his. He hadn't been able to stop thinking about what that meant. When Kara had handed him an envelope of cash, she'd given him more than money...she'd laid the first step on his road to claiming Jenna.

"When are you going to start the raised gardens?" she asked, setting their dinner on the table.

He sat. "Tomorrow, actually. I want to get them done before your vinyl comes in. Listen, even though I'm taking other projects, the café is my priority. Your project isn't getting back-burnered. I won't slack on my responsibilities here."

She gave him a reassuring smile. "I didn't think you would."

He removed the top of the plastic container and inhaled the scents of turkey and dressing. As they ate, he told her how Kara and her mother had both offered to recommend him. He hoped Jenna didn't mind that he'd used the café number for people looking to reach him and promised that he'd get a cheap cell phone soon. Though she insisted she wasn't concerned, he didn't like the idea of her taking messages for him. She had enough on her plate without him adding to it.

By the time he finished his dinner, his stomach was full and his eyelids didn't want to stay open. Jenna chuckled.

"Get in bed," she insisted as she put the containers back in the bag. "We'll catch up over breakfast."

He leaned back as she wiped the table clean. Seeing her here, being so comfortable, made his heart swell. His mind had been racing since they'd damn near kissed the other day. Every thought seemed to be about making a future with her. He'd never planned a future with a woman before, but he couldn't imagine one without her now. She rinsed the dishrag she'd been using, squeezed out the excess water, and draped the rag over the faucet before drying her hands.

As she gathered the reusable containers, he said, "Would this be enough for you?"

She stopped moving and looked at him.

He dragged his hand over his face. The question left him before he could stop it. "Sorry. I'm tired," he said.

"What do you mean by *this*?"

"Nothing. My mind was just wandering and my filter isn't engaged." He rubbed his eyes. "Working in the sun drained me."

She sat back down. "When I was at the culinary institute, I wanted to travel the world and learn all kinds of new techniques and foods to bring back here and apply to a restaurant. When I met Peter, I wanted to do whatever was necessary for him to succeed. When I got back here and opened the café, I just wanted to make a life for myself and run a business that wasn't upside down financially." She looked at her hands and bit her lip, giving him the distinct impression she wasn't done.

"And now?"

"Now, I find myself thinking about what could be if..."

"If what?"

She flicked her eyes at him, but didn't hold his gaze. "It's been a long time since I've had someone in my life. I'm kind of lonely, to be honest. When I came back, Marcus and Annie weren't even dating. He spent a lot of time here, helping me get the café started. But he's got a wife now. My customers are great, but I don't see them outside of the café. Hell, I don't see anyone outside of the café except for an occasional game night with Annie's family. And I'm the odd woman out there. Everyone is married but me." She drew a breath and bit her lip. "It'd be nice to have someone," she said softly. "Someone who didn't care that I don't have time to fix my hair or put on makeup or that I smell like cheeseburgers most of the time."

"I happen to like cheeseburgers."

She glanced at him and giggled, but her smile faded just as fast as it had appeared. "It would be enough for me. But I get a feeling it wouldn't be enough for you. I can't be with someone who doesn't think I'm enough. I did that once. Didn't end well."

"You are more than enough, Jenna. I'm the one who is lacking." He swallowed, debating for a moment before pushing himself up and grabbing his notebook. "Remember how I told you I wanted to be a builder like Charlie when I grew up?"

"Yeah."

He swallowed his pride, knowing she wouldn't laugh at him. She would never laugh at his goals. "I'm going to do it, Jen. I know having a few jobs lined up isn't the same as owning a business, but I can do it. It'll take time, I know that, but I have the skills and if I keep getting word-of-mouth referrals, I can build up a client base. I can't take on big projects like Charlie, but I can do roofing and raised gardens and things like that. Eventually, maybe I can get a small crew and do larger home repairs."

She ran her fingertips over his notes. "Maguire Construction. I like it."

"Yeah?"

She squeezed his hand. "Yeah. You know, we can set up a website. We'll post pictures of the café to show your work. Put a few ads in the paper and flyers around town. You'll have a list of projects before you know it."

His heart swelled at the thought, but as always, reality brought him back down. "I have to get a truck soon. I can't keep borrowing from Charlie. And I'll have to get better tools—saws and things like that."

She tightened her hold again. "One thing at a time."

Looking at the notebook, he blew his breath out. "The last two days of coming home with something to tell you about my day and with a job to go to tomorrow… It's given me hope. It's made me feel like a man again." He covered her hand with his. "I want every night to be like tonight. You and me talking about our days, making plans for the future. Just being together. That's what I meant when I asked if this would be enough for you. Would you be happy if this was our life?"

"I would be very happy if this was our life," she whispered.

"You'd want that with me?"

"Very much so."

That was all he needed. Standing, he pulled her up with him and cupped her face. He searched her eyes, watching for any sign of hesitation. "I promise I'll never make you feel like you aren't enough, because you are so much more than I deserve. I'll take care of you and protect you. You'll never doubt that I love you and *only* you. But you need to know that I'm jealous and insecure. I'll need reassurances. Loving me won't be easy, but I will do everything I can to make sure you never regret it."

Her throat moved as she swallowed. He was certain she was going to tell him to find someone else to burden with his brand of dysfunctional affection, but then a hint of a smile found her.

"I'll be timid. Indecisive. Scared. Submissive. I'll need you to be jealous and insecure and need reassurances because that will reassure me. I'll need you to protect me and take care of me because I find it really hard to do that for myself. Mostly..." She blinked a few times. "...never let me doubt that you love me, because I don't feel very lovable most days."

He put his forehead to hers and took a long breath. "Once you're mine, I won't give you up without a fight," he whispered. "You've gotta be sure you want this, Jenna. You've gotta be sure you want me."

She closed what little bit of space there was between them. "I want you, Daniel. Without hesitation. I want you."

He let out the breath he'd been holding and something like a small cry came out with it. "Then you're mine."

CHAPTER SEVENTEEN

*W*hen Jenna had said she feared Daniel would consume her, she had no idea how true that statement was. The moment she asked him to claim her, he'd growled low in his throat, pulled her against him just enough to lift her toes off the floor, and then she was on her back on his bed with him lying over her. That intensity that she'd come to know had returned to his eyes, but now she knew exactly what it meant—she was his and he was hers, and he needed to stake his claim. If only he knew how much she *needed* him to stake his claim.

She needed to belong to him. She needed him to own her in the way he feared would drive her away.

Holding her head, digging his fingers into her hair, he pressed his mouth against hers and shoved his tongue between her teeth and then nipped at her lips. Once he'd thoroughly tasted her mouth, he moved on to her neck. She tilted her head, exposed the flesh for him to explore with his lips and tongue. And he did.

He leaned back and she read in his eyes that he was saying... this was the point of no return. "Do you want me to stop?"

"Never," she breathed.

"I'll try to be gentle," he whispered.

"I didn't ask you to," she returned just as quietly. She'd been craving the taste of his mouth for so long, drowning in her need. Now that they'd given in, she didn't want him to hold back.

His breath left him in a *whoosh* and he crashed his mouth to hers again. She felt his erection against her and ground up into it. He responded, pressing to her, moaning as he did. He pushed himself to his knees, and in doing so pressed her thighs back and open. He discarded his shirt and reached for hers. She sat up enough to let him pull the fabric over her head.

A flash hit her. She was lying there on his bed in too-snug jeans that accentuated the pooch of her stomach. Her bra was tight, creating pockets of chub bunched above the band. How much he must have regretted wanting to see her naked.

"Stop," he breathed harshly. He ran his hand over her stomach, her breast, and then cupped her face. "You are perfect, and I couldn't possibly want you more than I do right now." He kissed her hard, distracting her from her self-doubt. "I want to worship you, but I think that's going to have to wait until next time. I don't have the patience right now. I need you so much, Jenna."

She rolled her head back as he lowered his kisses over her

neck and nipped at one peaked bud pressing against her old bra. But then he pulled back. She opened her eyes as he climbed off the bed. She would have protested if he weren't unbuckling his pants.

She toed her tennis shoes off and by the time they landed —*thud, thud*—on the hardwood floor she had planted her heels on the edge of his mattress. While he tore open a magically appearing condom, she unbuttoned her pants, pushed the zipper down, and lifted her hips so she could push them over her thighs. She barely had them to her knees before Daniel took over, yanking the denim away. As he tugged at her socks, she unhooked her bra and then he was on her.

His head was deep between her legs before she knew what was happening. She gasped, moaned, and damn near had a seizure at the feel of his tongue brushing over her. Sadly, he didn't linger.

"God, how I've wanted to taste you," he muttered as he moved up her body, cupping her breasts, flicking his tongue across each nipple before meeting her eyes. "Every inch of you." He gripped her hands and pressed them to the mattress, and then he was in her. One hard, demanding, *claiming* thrust.

She was his. He pulled back and then claimed her again, and she cried out his name.

She hadn't had many men in her life, but none had ever fit her so completely. So fully. None had ever made her feel so wanted just by moving inside her. His lovemaking was as intense as his stare. His weight held her in place, making her feel owned.

And getting owned by this man was the best feeling she'd had in a long time. He'd said he'd make her feel loved, and she did. In that moment, she thought she had never felt so completely loved in her entire life.

Tears bit her eyes and rolled free before she could blink them away. He hesitated, a spark of concern flickering on his face, but she tugged her hand free and pulled his head down, kissing him hard, silently letting him know she was fine.

He traced his hand down her side and grabbed her thigh, lifting her leg up and wrapping it around him. She slid her arms around his neck, completely giving in to him. Becoming his.

"Jenna," he whispered in her ear. "My sweet Jenna."

And she came undone.

Watching Jenna rest brought a sense of peace to Daniel he didn't think he'd ever experienced. She slept curled on her side, her mess of dark hair on the pillow next to his. He ran his hand down her side, marveling at the fact that she was really there. She'd accepted him and his broken soul. His conviction to succeed at his plan to start his own business grew. But so did his doubt. He had a few hundred dollars to his name from the roofing job. He'd earn a few more by the time he finished the raised gardens. But then what? People weren't banging down his door to ask him to work for them.

Rolling onto his back, he closed his eyes and rubbed his

fingers over the burning orbs. He needed sleep. But he was terrified.

The bruise on her head had faded, but his memory hadn't. What if he drifted off and she shifted next to him? What if she got up to use the bathroom and startled him when she got back into bed? He couldn't risk hurting her.

A quiet moan left her as she rolled onto her back. Her hand dropped onto his chest, and she jolted.

"It's me," he whispered.

She instantly relaxed, and then turned onto her side to look at him. "What time is it?"

He pressed the backlight on his watch. "Almost three."

She ran her hand over his chest and sighed, but then she gasped and sat up. "Shit. I never cleaned up the café."

He pulled her arm. "I did."

"What?"

"I couldn't sleep so I went down and cleaned up."

She sat. Not speaking. Looking down at him with shadows playing across her face.

"I've helped you enough, I knew what to do."

"It's not that."

He swallowed, worried he'd screwed up somehow. "What is it?"

She finally smiled. "This will be the first time I haven't ended my day by running a dishwasher in a very long time. Thank you." Lying back, she curled on her side next to him. "Why couldn't you sleep? Are you okay?"

"I'm good," he said, his voice gravelly from exhaustion.

His counselor said he was doing better. He was learning to reconcile his anger. He was losing some of his edge. He thought so, too. Peace was a bit easier to find these days. Usually in the café or having dinner with Jen. She was a balm for his soul. He doubted she had any idea how much she did for him, even if he had told her a thousand times.

She'd given him more than a project and a home. She'd given him a purpose and now she'd given him a reason to live. Stroking his hand over her back, he absorbed her warmth and listened to her breathe. Every soft exhale as she'd slept next to him seemed to heal him a bit more.

Even so, he couldn't ignore what had happened the last time she'd woken him.

"Babe?" she asked softly, bringing a smile to his lips.

He turned on his side so he could look at her and lightly brushed her hair back. "I was afraid to fall asleep. I didn't want to hurt you if something startled me."

Her brow creased and even in the dim light, he could see the distress in her eyes. "You've got to let that go."

"I'll never let that go."

"Daniel." She exhaled slowly, as if rethinking what she intended to say. "Do you want me to leave so you can sleep?"

"No," he said quickly. "No, I want you here."

"You have to sleep."

He caressed her face. Her skin was so soft, so warm, he wanted to touch every part of her. "I know. But I'm not ready for you to go." He slid closer to her, pulling her body against his, and she responded by curling into him. She fit so perfectly. He could hold her there forever. The image of her, baby on hip, hit him again. "Six months ago, my life was in shambles. I didn't know up from down. I feel like everything I've ever gone through was leading me to this moment." He frowned. "That sounds like a line, doesn't it?"

"It sounded beautiful to me." She trailed her fingers through his chest hair, tickling his skin as she went. He didn't mind. The sensation reminded him she was really there. "Will you do something for me?"

"Hmm?"

"Close your eyes."

"Jen—"

"Close your eyes and listen to me." She tilted her head back, so he did as she asked and let his sandpapery eyelids close.

"Six months ago, I was thinking about giving up the café. Hell, six weeks ago, I was ready to, but you've changed everything. And I don't just mean the paint and the pipes. I mean me. You've made me want to try harder, to keep going. I know when people find out about us, they're going to tell me it's too soon. That I don't know you well enough to care for you so deeply. But the truth is," she said softly, "I feel like I've known you all my life. Like I've just been waiting for you to find me. That sounds like a line, too. But it's true." She traced his jaw. "I hope when you say that we belong to each other now, you mean that for the long haul and not just until you get what you need from me and can move on. I've been on the losing end of that before. I don't know if I can survive it again."

He fought to open his eyes. He had to see her face. "I mean that we belong to each other for as long as we live. Ups and downs. Good and bad."

She smiled. "Good. Because I want to think about the future and I want to plan for the future and I need to know if those plans include you."

Covering her hand with his, he brought her palm to his lips and kissed her gently. "They do. Every day."

Her smile widened. "Close your eyes and think about the future and how wonderful it will be."

He hesitated before doing so. Then, taking a breath, he saw her again...the mother of the child he didn't even know if she wanted. But the warmth of seeing her there, in their imaginary home, soothed his worries, and he let the tension in his shoulders ease.

And then he slept.

CHAPTER EIGHTEEN

*J*enna was hoping for a quick escape, but Annie hit her with her penetrating gaze the moment she walked into the café. Kara smirked as they slid into a booth, and Jenna knew she was in trouble.

"Sit," Annie demanded as Jenna put menus on the table.

"I have tables—"

"Sit."

Sighing, she sat next to her sister-in-law—at least that way she could avoid her demanding eyes a bit more easily—and focused across the table on Kara. That didn't help. She was smirking just as much as Annie.

"Kara said Daniel helped her at her mom's house."

"Yes." She looked at Kara. "I hope he did a good job."

"He did a great job. He's very good with his hands."

The memory of his touch nearly took her breath away. "He's very talented at what he does."

"And handsome," Kara said. "Those dimples. *Mmm.*"

Annie said, "And I hear he is very protective."

Jenna sighed. "I figured Paul wouldn't make it out of the parking lot before he was calling you and Marcus."

"Dianna called, actually. She was very glad Daniel stepped in. Paul would have, of course, but it seems he wasn't needed."

Kara grinned as she lifted her brows. "So. The handyman is handsome, protective, and good with his hands. How is he in bed?"

Jenna didn't need a mirror to know her face immediately turned bright red...possibly venturing into shades of dark purple. She stuttered, shocked that her friend would be so damned blatant. But then again, not surprised at all. Restraint wasn't one of Kara's finer-tuned traits.

"Holy shit." Annie nudged her. "You slept with him."

"Annie," Jenna whispered, and looked around. No one was listening. Or seemed to care.

"You totally slept with him," Kara said and laughed. "Why are you so embarrassed? He's a doll."

She looked at Annie. "Since when do we discuss such private matters?"

She pointed to her head.

"If you use the brain-damage excuse, I'm intentionally burning your lunch."

The three of them were laughing when Mallory dropped into the booth next to Kara.

"Hey," Kara said, taking in her soon-to-be daughter-in-law's blanched face. "You okay?"

"What's wrong?" Annie pressed her daughter, all teasing gone from the table.

Mallory let her breath out slowly. "I don't know. As soon as I walked in my stomach rolled. It smells so..." She grimaced. "Greasy."

Jenna looked from Kara to Annie. Kara was the first to grin. Annie's came a bit slower, but they all seemed to be having the same thoughts.

"When did this start?" Kara asked.

"Literally, like, as soon as I walked in. I think I just need some fresh air. I need..." She stopped and put her hand to her mouth as her eyes bulged.

"No," Jenna cried as she lifted her hands, as if that could stop what was about to happen.

"Up, up, up!" Kara shoved Mallory from the booth and Jenna pulled her up to stand. Rushing her toward the restroom, she stepped aside and let the mothers do their job as she went for a glass of water and some crackers.

By the time she returned to the restroom, Annie was stroking Mal's hair and Kara had bent down to look at her face.

"Better?" Jenna asked.

"I'm sorry, Aunt Jen."

She handed Kara the water glass. "Don't you dare be sorry, kiddo. I'm so excited."

She creased her brow. "About me getting sick in your restaurant?"

"About the baby," Annie offered.

Mallory's eyes widened. "Wh-wh..." She looked at Kara, who nodded. "Whoa. That explains so much."

Jenna's heart swelled as tears filled Mallory's eyes. "Oh, this is a good cry, I hope."

"Good tears," she said, and sniffed. She looked at Kara. "Are you sure?"

"You're pregnant, sweetheart."

Jenna sighed as Annie nodded. This moment was so precious. Being here as her niece realized she was going to be a mother. As her sister and friend realized they were going to be grandmothers. Marcus was going to be a grandpa. She was so honored to be sharing in this.

But the moment stung a bit as well. She wanted so much to be a mother. Even if it did mean sitting on the floor in the café bathroom trying to ease a queasy stomach. She'd wasted so much of her life on Peter. So many years that she should have spent building the life *she* wanted instead of listening to his empty promises.

She passed the crackers to Annie with a wistful smile. "I need to check on things out there."

"Thanks, Jen," Annie said, too focused on her daughter to notice the shift in Jenna's mood. She was glad for that. And she was glad Mallory's upset stomach had disrupted the conversation that had been taking place.

Walking into the dining room, Jenna went straight to the coffeepot to refill mugs and offer reassurances that the customer who'd dashed to the bathroom was fine—just a bout of morning sickness. As she did, she had to wonder if Daniel had any desire to have kids. They'd never even talked about that. Not that they'd really talked about much.

She'd told him she wanted him. Let him make love to her. Promised that she'd be his. And once again, she'd done all those things without even asking if he wanted the same things she did. Evenings spent talking about their days and planning for the future—that was all they had agreed upon. But beyond his goal of establishing Maguire Construction, she didn't know if he wanted marriage and kids. If he wanted to stay in Stonehill or return to Atlantic City. She wouldn't give up her café and she wouldn't move away from her family. That wasn't even on the table, not that she thought he'd ask her to. But she wanted more than this café and his construction company, and she had no idea if he felt the same.

Way to go, Jen. Screw it all up again.

"Jenna?"

She turned and caught Daniel's concerned gaze. She'd been staring off into space and hadn't realized it. She offered him a warm smile. "Good morning."

His concern didn't ease with her smile as it usually did. "Are you okay?"

She put the coffeepot back and then went into the kitchen. It was too early for Scott to come in. She had him there for lunch and dinner rushes, but she could handle breakfast without help. They were there alone, so she didn't hesitate to grab his hand and pull him to her.

"Are you regretting last night?" he said quietly.

"No. I'm just..."

The worry in his eyes grew. "What?"

"When I married Peter, I thought we would have a family, but his career and his dreams never allowed for it. It's a good thing. Now that I know what he was really like, I know that's a good thing we never had children. But..." She bit her lip and drew a deep breath. "Last night, we talked about forever and the future and... That's all very romantic when we're in bed, but..."

"You don't believe me?"

"I just wonder if we even want the same things. We've never had that conversation. Mainly because we are blindly jumping into this thing. This future we promised each other. What does that look like in your mind?" She swallowed, waiting for his response.

He searched her eyes. "When I saw you with Kara's daughter on your hip, my heart dropped to the bottom of my stomach. I'd never realized how much I wanted a family until that moment. I can't shake that image of you with a baby on your hip. I need to make something of myself because I want that. I want *more* than that. I want a house in a good neighborhood. I want at least two kids because being an only child sucks. I want a dog, a big dog, not one of those fur balls that yip all damn day. And...I want all that with you." He tucked a strand of hair behind her ear. "I want you smiling down at a baby on your hip. But with my baby. *Our* baby. And I know this all sounds crazy and rushed, but—"

"Actually," she said, cutting him off, "it sounds really nice."

"Nice?"

"Perfect. But the reality is, this *is* crazy and rushed, Daniel."

He sighed. "Well, I can't support a family right now, but I'm working on it, so this is like a five-year plan."

"Five years?" She smiled. "Considering our ages, maybe we should shoot for three? I'd like to be around to see the kids grow up."

"Three it is. This is right. This feels right. I don't care if we're rushing. We want the same thing. We'll figure the rest out as we go."

Draping her arms over his shoulders, she tilted her head back to look up at him. Fear tugged at her, but she forced it down. Daniel *was not* Peter. He was not manipulating her. She knew in her heart the connection between them was real. She'd felt connected to him from day one, she'd felt safe with him, and that hadn't changed. She believed him when he said he wanted those things, and more importantly, she wanted them, too. With him. "Would you think I was crazy if I said I loved you?"

His eyes brightened. He pulled her against him and shook his head. "I must be crazy, too." Dipping his head down, he captured her lips in a possessive kiss, reminding her that he'd definitely staked his claim on her.

"*Whoa!* Call the fire department."

Jenna pulled back. Mallory stood at the kitchen door with

Annie and Kara beside her, the two older women looking smug as hell while the youngest stood with her mouth agape.

"Who's that guy giving Jenna mouth-to-mouth?"

Annie laughed. "That's your aunt's handyman, darling."

sh

Daniel looked down at himself as he followed Jenna to Marcus and Annie's front door. He didn't have the nicest of clothes, but he'd worn his best button-down shirt and jeans. They ran a realty company and always seemed dressed to impress. This was the best he could do and he hoped it was enough. Jenna had said it was enough.

In fact, she'd smiled, lifted her brows, and suggested they stay home instead. As much as he'd have liked to be wrapped in her body at the moment, if he intended to build the future he'd promised her—and he did—he had to win over Marcus.

Annie was already on his side. She'd teased him and Jenna mercilessly after catching them sharing that heated kiss in the café kitchen. But Daniel had seen how protective Marcus was of his sister.

"It's just Marcus and Annie, right?" he asked.

She smiled over her shoulder at him as she reached the door. "Yes. And I made him promise to be on his best behavior."

"It's never a good sign when you have to make someone promise something like that."

She faced him completely, ran her hand over his chest, and

then leaned up to kiss him lightly. "Breathe. Hard as he tries—and he will because he thinks it is his job to defend my honor—I won't let him corner you." She opened the door and stepped inside. "Hello?"

"In the kitchen," Marcus yelled in return.

They slipped their shoes off and headed deeper into the house. Daniel looked around the house, noting how out of place he was there. She turned and gave him one more reassuring smile before walking into the kitchen and sliding the cake she'd brought onto the counter. Her brother stood at the counter, seasoning steaks while Annie poured a bagged salad into a bowl.

She looked up and beamed. "I would have chopped this myself, but the last time I used a sharp knife I accidentally stabbed my husband."

"Accidentally my ass," he muttered.

She laughed as she set the now-empty bag aside. "Hi, Daniel."

"Thank you for the dinner invitation, Annie."

Jenna leaned over the steaks and inhaled. "What are you using?"

"Get the hell away from my steaks, Jen," Marcus ordered.

She made a face at him before moving around the counter to Annie. "What can I do to help?"

"Open the wine. Unless you prefer beer?" she asked Daniel.

"Actually, water is great for me."

Jenna pulled two glasses from the cabinet and filled them with ice water from the dispensers on the fridge before opening the wine bottle. She filled two stemmed glasses just a quarter of the way and handed one to Annie. The other went to where Marcus was rubbing spices into the raw meat.

"Leave me alone, Jen," he warned, and she laughed.

"He doesn't like when I watch him cook because he thinks I'm judging him."

"You are." Marcus dropped the steaks onto the preheated griddle on the stovetop, washed his hands, and faced Daniel. "I hear you came to Jen's rescue the other day. Thank you for that."

Daniel nodded. "She had the situation under control."

"Paul said you leaped across the dining room, ready to defend her," Annie said in that slow speech Daniel realized she only used for him.

"He's very protective," Jenna offered.

"So much so that you had to stop him from confronting the guy," Marcus stated. His tone had a bit of accusation to it that Daniel found too familiar. He sounded like Charlie.

"The man grabbed me," Jenna defended. "You would have wanted to confront him, too."

"Dianna was very impressed." Annie cut Marcus a look that her husband didn't notice. He was too busy staring Daniel down.

The tension in the kitchen dialed up a notch. This wasn't the greatest start to his first dinner with her family.

Instead of the slow, cautious tone she used when speaking to Daniel, Annie narrowed her eyes at Marcus. "Don't make me ground you."

Daniel chuckled, and Annie glanced his way. "I spent a good deal of my time in the army overseas," he explained. "I've developed an ear for various inflections. I can understand you just fine."

She beamed. "Good. It's really hard to speak so deliberately."

"No need," he assured her.

Jenna smiled warmly at him, but Marcus sighed and focused on the steaks.

"So," he said after flipping the meat, indicating the real questions were about to begin. "Why did you leave the military?"

"Don't start," Jenna warned quietly.

Marcus lifted his hands. "You told me to get to know him. How can I get to know him if I don't ask questions?"

This was inevitable. At some point, Jenna's brother would learn about Daniel's issues. According to his shrink, it was better to face uncomfortable situations head-on instead of dancing around them, hoping they'd go away. He manned up and said, "I was doing a security check at a refugee camp one night. Heard some muffled crying, not an unusual sound in those camps, but I suspected something was wrong. I went into the tent and found a member of our allied troop trying to rape a woman. I dragged him from her tent and beat the shit out of him. Instead of getting sent to prison, like the allied general wanted, I was charged with assault of an officer and discharged. I lost my pension and all my benefits."

The tension in the room tripled. Annie gasped, her eyes wide, but Marcus stared at him, as if gauging whether his story was believable. Jenna offered Daniel that supportive smile of hers.

"He's very protective," she said again.

Marcus crossed his arms. "So you got kicked out of the army because you beat someone up. And you said you lost your job with your uncle because you beat someone up. And, according to Paul and Dianna, if Jenna hadn't stopped you from going after her customer, you probably would have beaten him up, too."

"There's no probably about it," Daniel admitted. "He grabbed Jenna and my first instinct was to defend her. I won't apologize for that."

"And you shouldn't," Annie offered before focusing on Marcus. "They didn't find the guy who did this to me"—she gestured toward her head—"until *someone* saw him one day and tackled him."

Marcus frowned at her, clearly not appreciating that his wife wasn't supporting him in the point he was trying to make. "I'm just pointing out that there is a pattern here."

Daniel lowered his face and exhaled. "Look, I've made mistakes in the past. I know that. I'm working hard to overcome them."

"He's doing great," Jenna offered.

Marcus nodded. "Good. I hear you're staying in the vacant apartment." He looked at Jenna. "Kara told Annie. She told me."

Jenna didn't justify his obvious offense at not learning of this arrangement firsthand.

"So I guess wherever you were staying before must not have been furnished."

"He was staying with his uncle," Jenna said before Daniel could respond.

Daniel leaned on the counter. "Listen, Marcus, I care a great deal about Jenna. I don't blame you for being on the defense. You don't know me. I get that. It's admirable for you to want to protect her. But you don't need to protect her from me." He looked at Jenna and sighed. "I plan on being around for a long time, so you might as well learn the truth now."

"Daniel."

"I was staying with my uncle, but after I left his crew, I moved out of his house, too. I left by choice. He offered to let me stay until I found another place, but I didn't want to make an already awkward situation worse. So I took what I could put in my backpack and left."

"And where'd you go?"

Jenna rolled her head back and shook it.

"I've been trained to survive in every kind of wild environment you can think of. Surviving suburbia was a breeze."

"Jesus Christ, Jen," Marcus breathed as he closed his eyes and pinched the bridge of his nose. "He's homeless?"

"Oh boy," Annie said under her breath.

"He's the one who fixed the pipe. I tried to do it myself, but I screwed up and he heard me screaming and thought I was in trouble. He helped me out a lot before we came to an agreement."

Marcus dragged his palm over his face before putting his

hands on his hips. "He's homeless, Jenna! You're dating a homeless man!"

She clenched her jaw and let out a slow breath.

"Marcus," Daniel started.

Marcus put his hands up as if to soften what he was about to say. "Look, Daniel, I'm sure you are a nice guy and you seem to have the best intentions, but I'm not sure I want you around my little sister."

"Your *little sister* is thirty-six years old." Jenna's anger came through loud and clear.

"You're dating a homeless man who can't hold a job because of violent outbursts!"

"I think I can decide whom to date without your input, Marcus!"

"When are you going to stop being so goddamned naïve, Jenna? He isn't any better than Peter. Hell, he could be worse!"

The room suddenly felt like a vacuum. All the air was gone. Daniel's hackles went up. Annie put her hand on Jenna's shoulder as Jenna narrowed her eyes.

Marcus seemed to realize his mistake, because he leaned back and once again dragged a hand over his face. "I just mean—"

"I don't give a damn what you mean," Jenna seethed. "We're leaving."

She turned, but Daniel didn't follow.

He held his breath as she stormed from the room. Putting his hands on the counter, he exhaled. "You don't have to like me. You don't have to approve of the choices I've made or the steps

I've taken to rectify my mistakes. But don't ever throw Peter in her face again. She's still hurting over his betrayal. More than you could ever realize." He turned to Annie, who appeared as upset as Jenna, and bowed slightly. "Thanks again for the invitation. I hope next time will go better."

"That was so uncalled for," Annie said to her husband as Daniel left them alone.

At the front door, he grabbed Jenna's arm before she could reach for the knob and turned her to face him. Putting his hand to her cheek, he sighed as her lip trembled. "That wasn't about you. He doesn't trust me."

"He's never going to let me live that *one* mistake down. He had to bail me out, and he's never going to let me forget it."

"Jen," Marcus called. "Wait!"

She pulled from Daniel and jerked the door open.

"Let her calm down," he said as Marcus followed Jenna.

"Stay out of it."

Daniel sighed and stepped aside, stuffing his feet in his shoes as he did. He didn't doubt for a moment that Jenna could handle her brother; she might even have benefitted from giving him a bit of her mind before they left.

"I'm sorry," Annie said as she approached him. "He just worries about her so much."

"I get that, but what he doesn't get is how deeply her wounds run. Throwing Peter in her face was the worst thing he could do. It's going to take her a while to get over that."

"I know. Daniel," she said as he reached for the door. "You

hurt her and Marcus's big-brother act will be nothing. I'll kill you. And I'll get away with it." She tapped her head. "I have brain damage."

He offered her a slight smile. "Yes, ma'am."

He didn't hear what Jenna was saying, but the way she shoved against Marcus's chest before opening her car door and climbing in told him all he needed to know. Daniel didn't bother looking at the man; he just slipped into the passenger seat and held on while she peeled out of the driveway.

CHAPTER NINETEEN

"*Y*our brother is here," Sara announced, coming into the café kitchen.

Jenna ground her teeth. "I'm busy. Take care of him for me, please."

Sara stood beside her as Jenna focused far more than necessary on doing inventory on the morning's delivery. Finally she gave up counting crates of eggs and looked at her waitress.

"He said you'd tell me that. You guys fighting?"

Exhaling, she returned her attention to the eggs. "Don't worry about it. If he doesn't want to eat, he can sit there until he rots for all I care."

"Taking that as a yes," she said before disappearing through the swinging doors.

Jenna looked at her watch. Scott was late. Again. "Son of a bitch," she muttered.

"Yes, I can be."

Putting her hand on her hip, she turned to where her brother had entered the kitchen and glared. "Employees only. Get out."

"Jen." He frowned at her as he closed the distance between them. "You look like hell."

"You look like an asshole."

"Two cuss words in less than a minute. Is this the influence your new friend has on you?"

"You really want to start off with that?"

She focused on the order wheel. The damn thing squeaked whenever someone spun it. Annoying as hell, but it gave her a reason to step around her brother. After washing her hands, she yanked the order down, skimmed it, and then went to the fridge to get ingredients to make a turkey club sandwich and a side of fries.

"I'm sorry," Marcus said. "I didn't mean to embarrass you last night."

She laughed bitterly as she dropped several slices of bread into the toaster. "You didn't embarrass me. You embarrassed yourself by acting like some holier-than-thou jackass."

He wanted to argue. She knew he did. But he didn't. He didn't say anything. She rinsed two large potatoes and pressed them through the cutter. Taking the stack of sliced potatoes to the fryer, she dropped them in a basket and set the entire package in the hot grease before returning to the counter to assemble the sandwich.

God, she hated him. He knew exactly how to press her

buttons. He'd stand there all damn day if he had to. When she was thirteen, he came to tell her he was leaving to travel the world. She was furious, told him she'd never speak to him again, so he stood in the corner of her room for three hours before she finally cracked and laid into him for abandoning her. His silent brooding always ended with her losing her temper and yelling at him, and then him apologizing and her forgiving him.

Not this time. Hell no.

She put the sandwich together, pulled the fries from the grease, sprinkled her special seasoning mix over them, and then dumped them on the plate. She put the plate on the counter between the kitchen and the dining room and called out, "Order," to let Sara know the plate was waiting, and then turned her attention to cleaning up the mess she'd made.

She looked up when the back door opened. Her rage ignited when Scott strolled in—she glanced at the clock—forty-five minutes late. "No," she said, and he stopped in his tracks. "Just turn around and leave."

"What?"

"I told you the last time you were late that was *the last time* you'd come in late."

He scoffed. "You're firing me?"

"You fired yourself. Leave."

"Jenna."

"Get out, Scott. Go. Now."

He stared at her, setting his jaw as he narrowed his eyes. "Fuckin' bitch," he muttered as he left the way he'd come in.

"Jenna," Marcus said, clearly as shocked as Scott had been.

She turned on him. "You can leave, too. I don't need his shit any more than I need yours."

"Hey—"

"I am so fucking sick of being everybody's goddamned doormat. You treat me like a child, Marcus. You left when I was thirteen and somehow in your mind, I'm stuck at that age. Like I never grew up and can't figure anything out on my own. You think I don't know how badly I screwed up with Peter? You think I don't know I wouldn't be in this situation if I hadn't been so blind? I know! I know it every day that I scrape to get by. I don't need you reminding me of that, and I don't need some punk-ass kid making my life any harder than it is already. I don't care what you think about Daniel. I don't need you to approve or understand. I don't need you to trust him or believe that he cares about me. Because *I* do. You weren't there when I was with Peter. You have no idea how much he hurt me. All you see, all you understand, is that I blew through my inheritance for him. That I left school to be with him. He did so much more than take my money, Marcus. He broke me. Not just my bank account. *Me.*"

She swallowed, cursing herself for the way her voice cracked and the tears that made her vision blur. "As disappointed as you were in me, I was even more so, and I carry that with me every day. But for the first time in a really long time, I have someone in my life who sees beyond my mistakes and believes in me. I will not let you ruin that because *you* don't understand. Daniel has issues. I know that. But so do I."

Marcus reached out for her, but she turned when the order wheel squeaked again. Sara looked through the window, but quickly walked away.

"Lunch rush is starting. You need to go so I can focus on cooking."

"Let me help. I can cut fries or—"

"No. I just want you to leave. And don't come back until you're ready to give Daniel a chance."

She focused on the ticket that had just come in, but listened as Marcus sighed and finally walked out. A tear dropped, landing on the paper and smearing the ink. As soon as the doors stopped swinging, Jenna leaned on the counter and let several body-wracking sobs leave her. That was all she allowed. A few seconds of hurt, and then she drew in a deep breath and let it out slowly. Pushing down the emotions, as she'd become so accustomed to doing, she cleaned her face, washed her hands, and dug into filling orders as the lunch crowd rolled in.

"Jenna," Sara said through the window less than half an hour into the lunch rush, "I can't keep up. I need some help in the dining room."

She flipped two burgers. "I have food on the grill and in the fryer, Sara. Just do the best you can, okay."

"Jenna," she practically begged, "I'm alone out here. I need someone to bus tables."

She looked desperately at the timer on the batch of fries she was making and then checked the doneness of the food on the grill. "Two minutes, okay? I'll come out and clear some tables in two minutes."

As soon as she cleared the cooking food off the grill, she filled the plates, checked the ticket numbers, dashed the food out, and then hurried back to get a tub to dump the dirty dishes into. She dropped that into the sink and rushed through cleaning as many tables as she could before hurrying back to the kitchen to wash and take on the next set of orders. She pushed herself through the same cycle several times over the next hour and a half. Finally, the orders slowed and she could take a moment to breathe. She took in the messy kitchen and that same old feeling of being overwhelmed hit her. The sink was overflowing with dishes. Food had dropped all over the floor in her hasty preparation. Sweat soaked her T-shirt and hairline. And the shadow of her fight with Marcus was looming over her, pressing down on her spirits like a lead blanket.

She swallowed down her sense of desperation before it could consume her. She had just made one pass with the broom when the back door opened. Daniel stepped in and his face instantly fell.

Before he could demand to know what happened, she choked out a pathetic sound. "I fired Scott and kicked my brother out. The lunch rush was a disaster."

He was on her, his arms around her, and she had to fight the need to fall apart.

"Baby," he breathed. "You should have come to get me. I could have helped."

"How?"

"I don't know. Somehow." He kissed her head. "Give me this."

She didn't argue when he took the broom and started sweeping the floor. Sara came in with another pile of dishes. She looked around until Jenna took it from her. "I'll have help here tomorrow," she promised.

"I'm going to kill Scott when he shows up," Sara huffed.

"He did. I fired him on the spot. He won't be back," she muttered. Turning, she gave Sara a shrug. "Sorry. I just reached my limit when he showed up late again. That's the second time this week."

"I get it. I just don't want another day like today. I can't keep up with serving and clearing tables."

"I can clear tables," Daniel offered. "I can't do much else, but I can stay on top of the tables."

"That's all I need." Sara grabbed the disinfectant to wash tables and was gone.

"Thank you."

Daniel gave her a slight nod. "I'll sweep. You hit those dishes."

sh

Daniel thought he was going to have to carry Jenna up the stairs.

He would, too, if she needed him to. She was dragging, and not just physically. She hadn't offered him a warm smile once today. That was tugging at his heart in a way he'd never expected.

He locked the door as she started up the stairs. Cleaning up had taken a bit longer than normal since Jenna hadn't been able to do her usual upkeep throughout the night, but together they tackled the dining room and kitchen and stacked the clean dishes. She even chopped some vegetables for the morning omelets before giving in and telling him she couldn't stay on her feet one more minute.

Gripping her hips, he helped her climb to her landing. As soon as they were inside her apartment, he steered her to the bed.

"I need to shower," she moaned.

"You need to rest." He left her there as he went to the bathroom and started filling the tub. He returned and tugged her shoes off. "Now, I don't know much about spoiling women, but I hear hot baths go a long way after a hard day."

She sighed and closed her eyes. "You're the best."

He smiled as he tugged her socks off and then pulled her into a sitting position and kissed the tip of her nose. "I'm working on it."

She finally smiled at him, lifting heavy eyelids as she did. "Thank you for helping today."

He tugged her shirt up, lifting the image of Tony Danza over her head. "I'll always help. All you have to do is ask." He unhooked her bra, released the fastener on her pants, and pushed them along with her underwear over her hips. She put her hands on his shoulders as he kneeled down to help her step out of her jeans. When she was naked, he walked her to the tub. She sighed as she sank down, and he went to work on washing her, gently digging his fingers into her muscles.

"We didn't get much chance to talk today," he said.

A long breath left her. "I don't really want to talk about today."

"You fought with Marcus again?"

"He showed up with his empty apologies and I didn't want to hear them. I told him to leave."

"I don't want you fighting with your brother over me, Jen."

"We didn't fight over you. We fought over his inability to let me be an adult and make my own choices."

He lowered his gaze, focusing on her calf as he ran soapy fingers over her. "He's right, you know? I'm a homeless man who can't hold a job."

"Don't. Daniel, please don't. If you start getting down on yourself, I'll feel obligated to counter all your reasons, and I just can't right now. I'm too exhausted. Can we just be here? Right here, right now. We'll sort everything else out tomorrow. Please," she whispered.

"Okay. But we will talk tomorrow."

She closed her eyes and sank down in the water as a bit of a smile tugged at her lips. "Know what I want to do next? After the flooring and the vinyl."

"The plumbing and the electrical."

She chuckled. "After the plumbing and the electrical."

"What?"

"I want to take a day off. A real day off. Not half a day. A whole day. And I want to spend it with you doing absolutely nothing."

"I'll see what I can do to make that happen."

"I have to hire more help first."

"Until then, let me help."

She drew a breath and he couldn't help but look at the breasts breaching the waterline. She drew wet fingers over his cheek and in turn, he traced his hand over her stomach, then lower. She closed her eyes and gasped when he slid his hand between her legs. Parting her thighs for him, she moaned as he pushed two fingers inside her. When he pressed his mouth to hers, she panted against his lips, moved against his hand, and then breathed his name as her body gave in to him.

Then she sank below the water. When she emerged, she washed her hair and asked him to get her a towel. He helped her stand and dry and then scooped her up. She giggled as she wrapped her arms around his neck, but by the time he eased her onto the bed, her amusement was replaced by lust.

"You need to sleep," he whispered.

She pulled him down and kissed him. "I need a lot of things."

He wanted her to rest, but he wanted to feel her, too. She tugged his hand and his desire to feel her won. After coming home from Marcus's house the night before, she'd cried herself to sleep in his arms. He hadn't known what to do. All he could do was hold her and wish he had kept his mouth shut. He hated that Marcus had lashed out because of him, but he didn't think he was wrong. If he and Jenna had hidden the truth from her brother, he would have found out about Daniel's dishonorable discharge at some point. He'd have found out about his living situation at some point. If Daniel had lied now, the truth would have just seemed worse later.

So he'd been honest. Marcus had lashed out. Jenna had been hurt. She insisted she didn't blame him, that she understood why he had told her brother the truth, but that hadn't stopped her tears from falling.

He hadn't been able to pull her inside of him to protect her like he'd wished, but as he slipped between her legs and held her tight, he thought that was the closest he'd ever get. Moving slowly, gently, taking his time to feel her and let her feel him, was the best he could do. When she clung to him, whispered his name, and told him how much she needed him, he thought maybe she was right; maybe this was enough for now.

CHAPTER TWENTY

*T*he next day was considerably easier. Daniel got up with Jenna and they headed to the café together. Though she insisted he could sleep in and come down for lunch, he wanted to be there with her all day. She appreciated his effort more than she could have possibly expressed to him. He kept the floor and tables clean and she showed him how to run the dishwasher, which he did throughout the day, loading and unloading as needed to stay on top of the dishes.

By the time the dinner rush ended, she was tired, but not exhausted like she'd been the night before. Daniel had learned quite a bit during his first day "working" the café. She'd even looked through the window and caught him refilling coffee mugs without any prompting from Sara. He seemed so pleased with himself, it kept her spirits up all day.

She was surprised she hadn't seen Marcus come through the café doors today, but maybe he'd actually heard her and wouldn't interfere with her relationship with Daniel. Knowing he'd rather brood than try to make amends pissed her off, but she let it go. She wasn't going to let him get to her. Not when she had so much on her plate already.

Dropping into a booth, she dug into the tub of utensils and dropped a knife, fork, and spoon onto a napkin, expertly rolling them. She couldn't help but smile as she thought about the day. How perfect it had been to have Daniel there, working beside her. As he mopped the kitchen and she prepared the settings for the next day, she pictured this being part of that future they'd been discussing. Not that he'd want to give up his construction company to bus tables and mop floors, but she didn't think he'd ever be opposed to helping her at the end of a long day.

Knowing she had a man in her life who wanted to help her, who wasn't just out for himself, was an incredibly nice feeling.

She grabbed another set of utensils and just as she finished rolling the material, the glass in the front door busted. Jenna screamed, covering her face as another window broke. She threw herself to the ground, protecting her head and face as debris showered over the café floor. The sounds seemed to last forever—glass shattering and bouncing across the scuffed and cracked linoleum floor—and then there was deafening silence.

She swallowed as she eased up, looking around her. "My god," she whimpered. Every window along the front of the café lay on the floor in a million pieces. Tires squealing just outside jerked her from her trance. "Daniel," she breathed. Pushing herself up, she screamed out to him. She rushed into the kitchen.

The room was empty, but the back door was wide open. Damn it, he'd probably run after whoever had smashed the windows. "Daniel?" she screamed into the alley.

He didn't respond. He couldn't. He was lying face down on the old cracked asphalt.

8h

Goddamn. Daniel couldn't remember the last time his head had hurt so much. The attack north of Panjshir Valley—the one that left him so badly scarred. He jerked his eyes open, certain he'd find himself in a makeshift hospital with wounded soldiers and civilians all around him.

Instead, Jenna leaned over him, offering him a weak smile. Her nose was bright red and her eyes puffy. She'd been crying. A lot. Rage rolled through him and he didn't even know why. He just knew something had happened and he was pissed about it. She put her hand to his chest and shushed him when he tried to sit.

"Take it easy, Danny."

He looked to the other side. Charlie was there, looking worried as well.

"What happened?"

Jenna let out a shaky breath. "Somebody attacked you in the alley. Hit you with some kind of tool." Her voice cracked and her eyes filled with tears. "The doctor says you're fine. You just need some rest."

He exhaled as he closed his eyes, trying to grasp what she'd said. "Why would someone attack me?"

Jenna lowered her face but Charlie said, "The police are looking into it."

There was more to the story. So much more. He was going to press but the door opened and a police officer stepped in.

"Ms. Reid. Can I have a moment?" the police officer asked.

She offered Daniel that weak smile again before leaving the room.

"Charlie?" Daniel asked.

"I need you to think, Danny. Do you remember anything that happened in that alley?"

He closed his eyes. The last thing he remembered clearly was mopping the kitchen. "No."

"The police think you went out to dump the bucket and got attacked from behind. You fought back. Look at your hands."

Scuffs and bruises adorned his right hand. He'd gotten a few hits in before having his skull bashed. But he didn't remember anything.

"Who've you pissed off lately, Danny?"

He scoffed. Of course Charlie instantly blamed him. "Nobody."

"Whoever did this threw bricks through all the café windows. Jenna was there."

Rage boiled in Daniel's chest.

"I sent some of my guys over to put boards over the

windows, but damn it, Danny, that girl could have been hurt. If you know who did this, you gotta tell me."

He shook his head. "I haven't crossed anybody, Charlie. I've just been trying to get my shit together." He ground his teeth together when Jenna came back into the room.

"It wasn't him." She looked at Daniel, taking her seat again, and then frowned as she focused on Charlie. "I thought we agreed to let him start feeling better before you questioned him."

"You said," Charlie grumbled. "I didn't agree to anything."

She put her hand to Daniel's cheek. "Scott's alibi checks out. He didn't do this. The police are still trying to locate the man who was in last week—the one who grabbed me. There's a traffic camera just down the street, so they're going to check the footage to see if they can get a make on the car. The moneybag that I'd left on the counter with the morning's deposit was missing, so this could have just been a random robbery and vandalism. We don't know yet."

"The police think it was personal since you were attacked and the café was so badly vandalized. If you can think of anybody you've crossed, Danny—"

Jenna cut her gaze to Charlie. "We don't know anything yet," she said more forcefully.

Daniel found her hand and gripped her tightly. "Are you hurt?"

"No. Scared, but not hurt."

"Come here," he whispered.

She collapsed onto his chest. He hugged her close, buried his nose in her hair, and reassured himself she was safe. By the time he eased his hold on her, Charlie had left them alone. She took a few deep breaths.

"How's the head?"

"Not so great. You called Charlie, huh?"

"He's been sitting with me the entire time. Worried."

"He thinks I pissed someone off."

She shook her head. "The police think it was younger kids. You just happened to be in the alley so they hit you."

"Is that what you think?"

She bit her lip, clearly trying to fight her tears. "I have to because the idea that someone would do all this with the intent to hurt one of us terrifies me."

"You look exhausted."

"It has been a *long* day."

"What time is it?"

She glanced over her shoulder to a clock he hadn't noticed was there. "Almost four."

"In the morning? Have you slept?"

"No."

He winced as pain ricocheted around his skull when he moved, but he scooted over enough to make some space for her. "Get up here."

"Daniel."

"Jen. Come here."

She kicked off her shoes before climbing into the bed and putting her head on his shoulder.

Having her so close made his headache seem less intense. Her scent filled him, and he could breathe a bit more easily. "Are you sure you're not hurt?"

"Positive."

"I should have been there."

She chuckled lightly. "I'm sure you would have been if you hadn't been out cold in the alley." She brushed her fingers over his hand, the one with the wounds. "Did you happen to see who did this?"

"No." He closed his eyes.

"The police want to question you in the morning. The doctor wouldn't let them in tonight."

"I can't think of anything to tell them anyway."

"It's okay," she whispered. "They'll find who's responsible. And *they'll* take care of them."

He hugged her closer. Her warning had come through loud and clear. *Let the police handle this.*

He'd try, but he wasn't going to make any promises.

CHAPTER TWENTY-ONE

*D*esperation tugged at Jenna's heart at the sight of the café boarded up. She had no idea how long she'd be closed, but she knew it was going to take a toll on her bottom line. Business had just been starting to pick up. She was eternally grateful that Charlie had called in his crew to cover the windows, but she still had to call the insurance company. Once her agent had come and assessed the damage—which she hoped would be done quickly—she had to clean up the mess and replace the windows.

Her train of thought was derailed when Daniel unbuckled his seat belt. "Are you sure you're okay to climb the stairs?"

"My legs work just fine, babe."

"Well, if you fall, I can't catch you."

He smiled. "But it'd be fun trying, huh?"

She forced a chuckle for his benefit. He'd been trying to cheer her up since they'd woken with his doctor standing over them, ready to examine his patient. Daniel had a mild concussion and a cracked rib, but overall he was fine. The police questioned him, and he again said he didn't know anything—the last thing he remembered was being in the kitchen. He didn't remember fighting or getting hit or seeing the assailant.

Jenna hoped he wasn't lying. As much as she hated what had happened, she'd hate it worse if Daniel decided to exact revenge. The anger in his eyes was there for everyone to see, though he tried to hide it. She had just opened her car door when Marcus pulled up next to her. A knot formed in her stomach. She hadn't called him. Mostly because it was well after midnight before she'd had time and there wasn't a damn thing he could do.

He threw his sunglasses on the dashboard as he jumped from his car. "What the hell happened?"

She had told him the last time she'd seen him that she was tired of him treating her like the teenager he'd left behind when he moved overseas, but in that moment she became that kid again. Seeing him there, the one constant in her life, made her want to break down. She'd been strong for Daniel, determined not to make him worry more than necessary, but seeing her big brother rushing toward her instantly made her want to crumble.

He embraced her and she buried her face in his chest. "What happened?"

"The café was robbed and vandalized last night," Daniel said.

"Where were you?"

"Don't," Jenna warned, pulling back, her happiness at seeing him fading quickly. "He was hurt, Marcus. I had to call an ambulance. We're just getting home from the hospital."

His defensive stance relaxed a bit. "Sorry, I just..." He kissed Jenna's forehead. "Are you guys okay?"

"We're okay. I need to get Daniel upstairs to bed." She pulled from him and followed Daniel as he started up the stairs. She turned when Marcus went along. The determination on his face let her know his involvement in this wasn't an option. "Be nice," she whispered, "or go home."

He lifted his hands, indicating his surrender, but he scoffed when Jenna opened her door and ushered Daniel inside. She ignored him. "Do you want a shower?"

"Not yet."

"Get out of those clothes. They're filthy. I'm going to take Marcus downstairs and see the damage."

"I'll go—"

"The doctor said bedrest today." She put her hands on her hips and cocked her brows at him. "If you think for one second I'm going to disobey his orders, you are seriously mistaken."

"Jen, I've been hurt worse."

"Get undressed and in that bed. Now."

He stared her down before a grin twitched at the corners of his mouth. "Yes, ma'am."

"If I hear you moving around up here, I'm not going to be happy." She didn't care if her warning sounded more maternal than romantic. She'd spent half the night scared to death that his injury was more severe than it turned out to be. She'd spent hours imaging the worst. She needed to focus on the café now and worrying about him would only distract her. "Please. For my sake," she said more softly. "Follow the doctor's orders."

His amusement faded. "To the letter."

"Thank you." She headed for the door, stopping when Marcus didn't follow her.

"I'm glad you're okay," he said to Daniel, which was likely as civilized as she could have expected from her overprotective brother.

They were halfway down the stairs before Marcus asked, "Still mad at me?"

"Yes, but I have bigger problems today."

"You wanna tell me what happened now?"

The mop bucket still lay overturned in the alley. "I was rolling napkins and then all hell broke loose. The windows started breaking and glass was flying everywhere. When it was done, I sat stunned for a few seconds and then realized Daniel was in the kitchen. He had to have heard all that and there was no way he wouldn't have come running. I found him right here. Face down. I thought he was dead." She swallowed. "Everything after that is kind of a blur. They took him away in an ambulance and I called his uncle to go to the hospital. The police wouldn't let me leave until they finished questioning me." She put her hand to her head as she remembered the events playing out like a nightmare. "I had the deposit ready to go. The bag was sitting on the counter by the door when I went into the diner. I always set it there so I don't forget it. It was gone."

"Scott?"

She shook her head, blinking away the images of police snapping photos and looking for clues in the alley. "No. They questioned him. He had an alibi." She reached for the mop bucket but Marcus waved her hand away.

"I got it."

Once inside, she frowned at the mess. The police had dusted for fingerprints on the door and counter. The powder remained where the officer had sprinkled it. Marcus pushed the bucket into the closet and followed her as she went into the dining room.

"Holy shit," he breathed.

The room looked worse with daylight streaming through the few remaining windows.

"You were in here?"

She pointed to the corner table where her chore sat unfinished. "There."

He pulled her into a one-armed side hug and put his cheek to the top of her head. "You're so lucky you weren't hit with one of those bricks."

She simply nodded. She had a few scrapes from the glass that rained down on her, but nothing worth worrying anyone about.

"They don't know who did this?"

"Not yet. They think it was probably random. Daniel warned me about this a thousand times."

"What?"

"My routine. How easy it was to do something like this. He said I was too predictable. Made myself a target."

"He said that to you?"

She turned, frowning at the anger on his face. "Before this happened. He's been saying it for weeks. He tried to tell me how vulnerable I was making myself. I listened, but I didn't really get it." A flat laugh floated from her. "I get it now."

"Nothing about what you were doing brought this on, Jen. If this was about robbery, someone would have snagged the moneybag and run. This was personal."

She glanced at him, clearly hearing the clip to his tone. He was blaming Daniel. She wasn't going to argue with him. Not now. "I need to call my insurance agent. Hopefully he can get out here today so I can clean this up."

"I'll make some calls about getting the windows replaced."

"Actually, Daniel's uncle is doing that today. He's going to come by later with a few quotes." She sighed at the put-out look on his face. "He owns a construction company, Marcus. His guys rolled out of bed in the middle of the night and boarded up the windows. They're good people."

He exhaled and nodded. "I'm not used to other people helping us out. That's all."

She softened. "Us?"

"Annie...well, you know Annie."

She laughed softly. Yeah, she knew Annie. Never afraid to speak her mind and set people straight.

"She had a thing or two to say about what happened at dinner."

"Like what?"

"She says I'm pouting because Daniel's taking my place as your go-to guy. Maybe I am a little. This place brought us back together. When I got back to the States, you were already off to school in California. And then you married Peter and you know how I felt about him. I was always your hero when you were a kid, Jen. It was nice to have you need me like that again. I guess seeing that you had someone else here to help out stung me a little bit. But you were right, you're not thirteen anymore and you can think for yourself. I'm sorry I threw that jackass in your face."

She nodded. "Forgiven."

"Just…" He sighed. "God, Jen. Be careful with Daniel. He seems like a lit fuse just waiting to go off."

"He's had a really rough life, Marcus. His father was abusive, his mother died when he was young. He joined the army to get out and he found his place only to lose it because he pissed off the wrong person. He's struggling, but he's finding his way."

"He's got a lot of anger in him."

"I know, but he's working on it and I trust him completely. He will never turn that anger on me. Give him a chance. Please. He means a lot to me, and I don't want to feel stuck between you."

He nodded. "I will. I'll give him a chance."

She smiled, probably her first real smile since she'd had a

falling-out with him. "Thank you."

He nodded. "I tell you, though, I feel sorry for the poor soul who destroyed your café if Daniel finds him before the police do."

"Yeah." She watched sparkles dancing across the floor as light reflected off all the chunks of glass. "Me too."

Daniel's head felt much better as he drifted from the nap he hadn't meant to take. Jenna might have insisted on bedrest, but he had planned to lie back just long enough to appease her before going to assess the damage to the café. He'd passed the hell out. Apparently she'd been right; he wasn't quite as tough as he thought.

The sun was lower in the sky, indicating he'd slept the afternoon away. A quick glance around her apartment confirmed he was alone. Rolling to sit, he moaned at the immediate throbbing in his head. Jenna had left the samples of extra-strength aspirin the doctor had handed her sitting on the nightstand with a glass of water. He swallowed two down, chased the pills, pulled his jeans on, not bothering to button them, and then went up to his apartment. After a quick shower, he put on clean clothes and headed down to the café, where he suspected Jenna was.

He followed the voices trailing from the dining room. He stopped in his tracks as he stepped through the swinging door.

The last time he'd seen a room looking like this was when his team went in to help clean up a blast zone.

Charlie's voice came back to him. *"Jenna was there... Damn it, Danny, that girl could have been hurt..."*

He met her gaze. She'd stopped talking. She and the man next to her were staring at him. He swallowed.

"I just need a few more pictures," the man finally said. "Then I'll get out of here and you can clean up."

"Thanks." She crossed the room and touched Daniel's cheek. "How are you feeling?"

"Better."

"Hungry?"

He smiled. "You're always trying to feed me."

"It's what I do."

He hugged her to him, looking at the glass confetti that covered the floor. "How's your day?"

She moaned and shook her head. "This has been awful."

"I'm sorry I slept through it."

"You couldn't have done anything anyway."

"I could have been here. Come on." He pulled her into the kitchen and went to the fridge. "Turkey sandwich?"

"I was going to fix you something."

"I know you were. I want to take care of you."

"Marcus actually just left when the insurance guy showed up. He had postponed a meeting at his office, but needed to get to it. We worked things out."

"I'm glad." He turned with his arms full of sandwich meat and toppings to find she'd already set out two plates and was pulling bread out of a bag. "I was fixing you something to eat."

She grinned. "I like when we work together." She nudged him gently. "Last night had been going pretty darn well until the whole robbery-slash-assault-slash-vandalism thing."

He couldn't help but smile. "Yes, it was. I seem to remember thinking that before I blacked out." He nudged her the same as she'd done to him when he noticed her wistful smile had fallen. "I'm okay, you know?"

She squeezed her eyes shut and let her breath out. "You have no idea how scared I was finding you like that. My heart dropped to the pit of my stomach. We talk about the future and three-year plans, but in that moment…" She turned and rested her hip on the counter. "I'd be devastated if anything happened to you."

"I feel the same."

She glanced over her shoulder when someone knocked on the back door. He put aside the package of turkey as she opened the door. "Hey, Charlie."

He nodded but didn't return Daniel's smile. "How you feelin'?"

"Better. What's up?"

"I wanted to be the one to tell you."

"What?"

He glanced at Jenna. "When I got to the worksite this morning, I noticed some bricks missing from the stack that had just been delivered."

Daniel stiffened.

"Just a handful. Nothing that probably would have even caught my attention if it weren't for what happened here last night."

"I'm not following," Jenna said.

"Joel Taylor heard me talking the other day about how I was ordering supplies for the café to help you out, Danny. He's been real outta sorts lately. His wife left him and I sent him home yesterday for drinking on the job. He smarted off about how if he was my nephew, he'd get a truck and tools to play handyman. He's still real mad at you for confronting him."

Daniel clenched his fists.

"Now I'm not saying he did this, but I called the police officer who gave me a card. They came and looked at the bricks and confirmed they matched what was thrown through the windows. They're tracking Joel down now."

"Motherfucker," he said through clenched teeth. He needed to hit something. Or someone, actually—that wife-beating son of a bitch. He'd crack his fucking skull open.

"Are you saying that man Daniel lost his job over did this?"

"I don't know, but..."

"I know," Daniel barked. "He wanted to get back at me. This is just the type of passive-aggressive bullshit he'd do, too."

"Passive-aggressive?" Jenna asked. "You were attacked."

"From behind. He hit me over the head, Jen. I don't have any mark on me other than a few scrapes on my hand from fighting back. It wasn't a fair fight. That bastard doesn't know how to fight fair."

He started for the door, but Jenna grabbed his arm and Charlie planted his feet, lifting his hands to stop him.

"I don't know that it was him, but the police are handling it. And you're going to let them, Danny. You've come too far to screw things up now."

"Daniel, please," Jenna softly pleaded. "Don't do something stupid."

He clenched his fists and his jaw and every other muscle in his body followed. He was wound up and ready to even the score. "He destroyed your restaurant because of me."

"We don't know anything yet."

Closing his eyes, he exhaled and looked away. He knew. He'd brought this down on her. She'd paid for his mistake. She'd suffered because of what he'd done.

"I came to tell you so you wouldn't go off when the police get here and question you, Danny. You keep your cool and you answer their questions and you bite back any dumbass notion you have to make threats. You've been lucky so far, but if you lose your temper with the cops you'll be in jail. You hear me?"

A new layer of desperation touched Jenna's voice. "Daniel. Listen to him." A car door slammed in the alley and she pulled at his arm. "Stay calm."

He swallowed, tried to bury his anger, and nodded. He'd stay calm. He'd keep his cool. But that didn't mean he was any less inclined to hunt Joel Taylor down and put that pissant in his place.

CHAPTER TWENTY-TWO

*J*enna ran the shop vac Charlie had lent her over the last booth in the dining room. She was as confident as she could have been that no shards of glass remained ready to cut an unwitting customer. Charlie had saved the day more than once. First sending guys over to cover her windows, then giving Daniel a heads-up about his suspicions as to who had attacked him and vandalized the diner. Then he'd shown up with this super-powered vacuum to make cleaning easier. She was so glad that he and Daniel were repairing their relationship, and not just because it was helping her. If Charlie hadn't come here and warned Daniel that the police would be along to question him and why, Daniel probably would have lost his temper.

Instead, he'd answered their inquiry without incident. He'd been noticeably distant since, though. He wiped a rag over the counter for what she thought could have been the hundredth time. His body was there, but his mind was a thousand miles away. She wanted to ask him, but didn't think she really wanted to know. Guilt hadn't stopped playing across his face since the police left.

Though the police had yet to find Joel Taylor and confirm his innocence or guilt, Daniel had already convicted the man. As Marcus had pointed out earlier, heaven help the man who did this if Daniel found him before the police.

Pushing the shop vac aside, she crossed the dining room and smiled at him. "I feel as exhausted as you look. I don't say this often, but we are ordering pizza tonight. You like pizza, right?"

"Sure."

She didn't bother asking him about toppings—he'd just tell her to order what she wanted anyway—so she got everything, figuring they could each pick off what they didn't want. The weight of his silence as they locked up the café and walked to her apartment was nearly suffocating. He sat on the bed and took one of the pills the doctor had given to him.

God, she hoped his mood was just his head aching. She feared it was more, so much more. Kneeling behind him, she put her hands to his shoulders, gently kneading as she looked at the stitches in his scalp. "Gonna be a heck of a scar to add to your collection."

He laughed softly but didn't answer.

Sliding her arms around his neck, she kissed his ear. "You okay?"

"Got a lot on my mind."

"Wanna share?"

He sighed heavily. "This is my fault."

She bit her lips to stop her exacerbation from leaving them. "No. It's not. And I don't blame you. Not for a moment have I blamed you."

"Doesn't make it any less so. He came after your café because he found out I was here."

"You don't know that."

"I do, Jen."

"So what if he did? That was his choice. His decision. Vandalizing my business, assaulting you, stealing my money... those were his choices."

"You were on his radar because of me."

She finally let the heavy sigh building inside her leave. Leaning back, she moved to sit beside him. "Do you know how long it took me to realize Peter's actions had nothing to do with me and everything to do with him? Years. *Years*, Daniel. I beat myself up for years, and I can't deny that sometimes I still do." She slid off the bed, kneeled in front of him, and took his hands. "No more. I'm not going to take blame for his actions anymore. And I don't want you taking blame for your father's actions. Or for this Taylor guy's actions anymore. We have to let go of all the things we couldn't control because if we don't, then they just control us, and I'm not going to let the past control me anymore. You can't let it control you either."

"It's not that simple, Jen."

"We've got a plan, Daniel. A future we promised each other.

We can't look at the future if we focus on the past." She stroked his head. "Why do I feel like I'm losing you right now?"

"You're not," he whispered.

"Your eyes say something different."

He cupped her face and pulled her in for a tender kiss. "I love you, Jenna."

Her heart should have soared at his admission, but instead felt like a rock in her chest. "I love you, Daniel."

He pulled her into another, much deeper, kiss, which she broke with a curse at the sound of footsteps on the stairs. Digging in her purse, she pulled out cash just as the deliveryman knocked on her door. After accepting the box and telling the kid to keep the change, she dropped the pizza on the table.

Daniel was on her before she could lift the top. His arms circled her waist and his lips covered her neck. She turned in his arms, capturing his kiss with her mouth. He was frantic as he pulled her shirt up and tugged at her jeans. Within moments, the pizza lay forgotten as he lifted her off her feet, pulling her legs around him. She clung to him as he took several steps and pressed her back to the wall, and then he was in her, thrusting hard and fast, and any fear of him leaving her was gone.

She was his. She knew that. She was stupid to doubt him. As he panted her name, she pulled him even closer, deeper. She cried out as her body responded to him—oh, how he had a way of making her respond. His teeth nipped at her neck as he rammed himself deeper one more time. He stilled and the only sound was their heavy breathing. After a moment, he leaned back and kissed her lips.

When she opened her eyes and met his gaze, her heart nearly stopped.

He hadn't been reminding her of his claim on her. He hadn't been promising her the future they'd spoken of.

He'd been saying good-bye.

sh

Daniel offered the gentlest smile he could muster when Charlie's wife answered the door. "Hi, Lisa."

"Daniel. How's your head?"

He laughed softly. "Been better. Charlie around?"

"Yeah. Come on in."

He stepped inside and waited by the door while Lisa went into the kitchen. A minute later, Charlie appeared. The curiosity on his face faded to disappointment.

"Leaving, huh?"

Daniel shifted the pack on his back. "Just for a while. I'll be back."

"When?"

"When I don't want to kill Joel Taylor." He smiled weakly but it didn't last. "When I can give Jenna what she needs."

"Seems like you have. She's pretty smitten."

"I want a life with her, Charlie. I told her we'd have a life. But...I'll just blow it if I keep ignoring all the things you've been warning me about. I need to get my head right before I get too deep with Jenna."

"She know you're leaving?"

"Yeah. She's pissed as hell, too."

"Rightfully so. You got her hopes up awfully high."

Daniel lowered his face. He'd never forget the pain in her eyes as she realized what he was thinking. "I'm coming back. I told her I'd be back."

"And what'd she say?"

"She told me you and her brother were right about me. I wasn't worth the trouble."

"Ouch, huh?"

"Yeah."

Charlie stood there for a few seconds. "You want to stay here?"

"No. That's why I'm here. I want you to help Jen with her café. Fix the windows and the booths and floor like we planned. I trust you to take care of her. To be fair and do a good job."

He nodded. "She loves you. Should have seen how scared she was at the hospital."

"I love her, too."

"So stay. I'll help you, Danny. I see you've been trying. I meant it when I said I'm proud of you. Stay."

He swallowed. "I can't keep pushing this anger down. It's going to get the best of me. Hell, it almost did when you told me your suspicions about Joel. I would have ended up in jail if you hadn't warned me. I would have lost it and gotten myself in trouble. Jen doesn't need that. I keep swearing I'll never hurt her, and I wouldn't, but my actions toward someone else did. My bad karma came back and kicked her feet from under her. I can't let that happen again."

"Did you tell her that?"

"Yeah. She told me I'm a coward who is looking for a reason to run."

"Is she right?"

"No. She just doesn't know how deep my anger runs. If she did, she'd be the one running. But I'm going to fix it, Charlie. Then I'm going to be back. Until I am, I need you to take care of her."

He laughed quietly. "You've got a hell of a way of getting me in the damnedest situations, boy."

"Yes, sir. I do."

"I made a promise like this to your mama. I don't think I did such a great job for her, but I'll do better for you. Jenna will be in good hands until you come back."

Hefting his pack higher on his shoulders, he felt the knot in his gut tighten. With a nod of thanks, he turned and walked away, taking the first step to leaving the past behind so he could embrace the future. He just hoped Jenna would be willing to embrace him when he returned.

he mailman set a package on the counter and a pang
of anxiety shot through Jenna. Right around the
first of every month for the last five months a package arrived.
The first time had been a surprise. No return address. No note.
Just a vintage Fleetwood Mac tee inside. She'd known it was
from Daniel even without a letter. Hope had found her. He was
thinking about her. Remembering her. Planning to keep his
promise to return even if she had been mad when he walked out
on her.

Mad didn't really cover it. He'd set her feet on the floor after
making passionate love to her and she'd made one final appeal
for him to stay. He rebuffed her plea and all the anger and
frustration of the days before erupted. She'd had a fight with
Marcus, her café had been vandalized, Daniel had been hurt, and
then, to top it off, he was walking out on her. Everything
collapsed around her and she stood naked, screaming at him to

leave and just forget about coming back, forget about his stupid three-year plan. Forget her, because she never wanted to see him again.

And then she'd finally given in to the stress and cried and cried, and the next day when she realized he really was gone, she'd cried more. Marcus was furious. Annie was sympathetic. Charlie was apologetic. And Jenna had been humiliated.

Everyone had told her so. Everyone had warned her. But she'd insisted she knew better, she believed in him, she trusted him. And that got her nothing. Well, not nothing exactly.

The first package had given her such a thrill, but as the months went by, they seemed to sting more than anything. Did he really think this was enough? A once-a-month reminder that he'd reneged on their plans? On all his promises? Five months later, the thrill was gone, and she was determined to leave all things Daniel Maguire in the past and embrace the future she was making for herself without him.

She eyed the package for a good fifteen minutes before finally giving in and opening it. As always, the contents only confirmed that he was alive and had become proficient at shopping for old T-shirts, this one for Meat Loaf. She chuckled as she sat on a stool.

Daniel had always liked her meatloaf.

Her shoulders slumped. He was making it impossible to let him go and she had to let him go. For her own sanity. She couldn't keep letting him stab at her heart like this—month after month.

Stuffing the shirt back in the box, she tucked it behind the counter and grabbed a coffeepot. She focused on refilling mugs and serving orders and wiping tables. When the crowd slowed, she hid in the back room and took inventory. Counting containers of spices was much better than remembering Daniel's smile. Hearing him laugh. Feeling his touch.

"Bastard," she breathed when he crept into her thoughts again. She moved on from inventory to menu planning. And when the café was empty and her staff had gone home, she focused on wiping down tables and booths and mopping the floor she still loved to admire. Charlie and his crew had done an amazing job.

She'd been closed for a week after the vandalism. In that week, Charlie and his crew came in, replaced the windows and floors, and reupholstered all the booths and stools. By the time she opened, it looked like a brand-new café and she'd been grateful for that. Fewer reminders of Daniel.

"Get out of my head," she muttered. She used to save that command for Peter's memory, but he didn't come to her mind much these days. No, these days she reserved it for Daniel.

When the floor was clean and the last round of dishes done, she turned off the lights and tucked the morning's deposit into the safe—she no longer carried it with her upstairs. Opening the kitchen door, she skimmed the now well-lit alley before stepping out. Another project Charlie's crew had done the week after Daniel had been attacked. The once dim alley was now as bright as noon on a summer day.

Summer was gone now, though, and she reminded herself again that she needed to start wearing a coat as she stepped out and turned to lock the door. The air wasn't cold but the warmth of the day was giving way to an autumn chill. She was halfway to the stairs before she noticed a figure sitting on the first few steps. Her heart dropped and she froze, ready to turn and run until she caught the man's dark gaze.

Daniel.

She was immediately snared in his intense stare and that familiar feeling of not knowing what was going on in his mind returned. She hated that feeling. But she also loved it, loved his intensity.

She hated how much she had missed that feeling of free-falling that he tended to bring to her.

"Hey," he said quietly.

"Hey."

He smiled, but his eyes seemed unsure. "How are you, Jen?"

She snorted and shook her head. "Oh, the usual, Daniel. Feeling abandoned and betrayed and manipulated by the man I thought I loved. How are you?"

He looked at his hands for a moment before nodding. "The usual. Ashamed, insecure, more than slightly dysfunctional. But happy to see the woman that I *do* love."

"What are you doing here?"

"I told you I'd be back."

"Mmm. Right. You backed out on everything else you promised, but *that* I was supposed to believe."

He stood and took the few steps to stand right before her. "I'm sorry for leaving, Jenna. But I had to."

"I know." She'd needed some time to come to terms with his decision, but she knew why he'd left. Charlie had told her a hundred times how torn up Daniel had been, but that he'd finally accepted that his anger was something he couldn't simply control. And though he knew, as Jenna did, that he'd never hurt her, he had hurt others and that wasn't something he wanted to bring into her life. She was still angry with him for cutting her out of his healing process, but she understood his decision. She'd had to come to terms with the pain Peter had caused her on her own. Nothing Daniel had said or done could heal that wound for her.

"Joel Taylor confessed," she said. "He pled guilty to all the charges brought against him. He'll be in jail for a long time."

"Good. That's good."

"Yeah, it's good." She crossed her arms and stared at him. "Are you going to tell me where you've been?"

"I went to DC. Tracked down a friend of mine who works at the State Department and asked him to help me appeal my dishonorable discharge."

"You can do that?"

"It's not easy. But...believe it or not, I actually don't piss off every person I meet."

She chuckled softly.

"I saved his ass in Iraq once. He's high enough on the food chain that he has some pull. He jumped through some hoops, pulled some strings, called in a few favors, and got my pension and benefits reinstated. I'm no longer listed as dishonorable."

She smiled at the pride illuminating him. Mad as she was at him, she knew how deeply the label had cut him. "That's great, Daniel. Congratulations."

"Yeah. It's amazing. Um, he also got me enrolled in a veteran's program that helped me learn some anger management. I can't say I'm cool and collected all the time, but it takes a lot more to set me off these days." He smiled. "Baby steps."

She swallowed some of her nervousness. "Yeah. Baby steps."

"I know I left a mess behind when I walked away, Jenna. I had to fix myself before I could go any further with you. I wasn't leaving you. I was protecting you from me. You know that, don't you?"

She bit her lip and diverted her gaze again. "Five months, Daniel. Not so much as a phone call in five months. Nothing but those stupid shirts. What the hell was that about anyway? A shirt but no note? What was that supposed to mean?"

"I wrote you a thousand letters. They just all sounded so pathetic I couldn't bring myself to send them, but I needed you to know you were on my mind." He put his hand to his heart. "You were always with me."

"Why no return address?"

"Because I didn't want you to come looking for me. I told you I'd be back."

"You told me a lot of things," she whispered.

"I meant every single word." He took a few steps, closing the distance between them. He didn't touch her, but she could feel him all the same. He'd caressed her face so many times she'd never forget how he felt. He searched her eyes. "You, the future I promised you… I thought about you every day. Every minute. My military appeal was hell. This anger-management program has been hell, but I pushed through because I knew…or I hoped…you'd be waiting on the other side. I know I hurt you and I'll never be able to tell you how sorry I am, but it was better to walk away from you to fix myself so I didn't hurt you worse later. I had to heal so my hurt didn't hurt you and our future."

She lowered her face, swiped away a tear, and shook her head slowly. "You should have called, Daniel."

"I'm sorry. Can I show you something?"

Before she could answer, he took her hand and led her toward the entrance to the alley. "Where are we going?" she asked.

"It's a surprise. Something I've been working on while I was gone." He pulled her through the alley to where he'd parked in front of the café.

She gasped as she finally realized what he was showing her. "Daniel!" She walked to a white truck and stared at the logo for Maguire Construction on the side. Damn him for making her heart swell. The last few months she'd been cursing his name at every turn and he'd been working so hard to better himself. Of course, if he'd called, even once, she'd have known that.

"You did it," she said when he stepped next to her.

"I borrowed against my retirement to get the ball rolling on that three-year plan of ours." The insecurity returned to his eyes. "I never forgot our plans, Jen. Everything I've been doing was to make that life for us."

She closed her eyes and sighed, and then looked at the truck again. "This is great."

"Well, I don't have any clients yet, but I just got back to town, so..."

"You'll get new clients in no time."

"I'm going to go see Charlie tomorrow. Let him know I'd like to take on some of the smaller projects he passes on. Maybe he'll refer me to some people."

"I'm sure he will. He's been so worried about you."

He lowered his face. "I never meant to worry anyone. I just couldn't seem to find my footing and I didn't want to drag you down."

"I get that."

"I, um, I peeked in the café before walking around back. Charlie did a great job. It looks amazing."

"Yeah, he's been great."

"And the lighting in the alley. That's good."

She nodded. "He's gone above and beyond. Have, um...have you talked to him lately?"

He shook his head. "Not since I left. You're not the only one I have to beg forgiveness from."

Taking a breath, she looked around the empty street. "You'd

spent your life working for something that was yanked away from you and you found yourself on a downward spiral. I understand that. I've been there. I know how hard it is to bounce back when you've lost everything." She swallowed hard and cut her gaze to him. "But you promised I'd never doubt that you loved me. And then you left me." She didn't bother to wipe away the tear that dripped down her cheek. He needed to see how much he'd hurt her. "Made me give up on you. Made me believe I'd made another huge mistake."

"Jen," he whispered.

"You made me look like a fool," she said before he could try to talk her out of giving him the verbal lashing he deserved. "I believed in you. I vouched for you with my brother and with Charlie. I told everyone that I could trust you. That you weren't the man they saw. That you were so much more. And you left me when I needed you the most. Once again I'd put all my faith in the wrong person and I was left holding an empty bag looking like an idiot."

He sniffed as he ran his hand over his hair. "I'm sorry." His tears didn't fall, but she could see the sheen in his eyes glimmering in the streetlight. "I'm so sorry. I don't deserve a second chance, Jenna. I know I don't, but I came here to beg for one." He grabbed her hand and kissed it once, twice, and a third time before holding it to his heart. "I've worked so hard to be better. For you. For this life I promised you. Please let me give it to you. Please let us have the home and the family that we dreamed we'd have. Please. Just give me a chance."

She looked away and he cupped her face, wiping her tears away with his thumbs.

"You don't have to decide right now," he whispered. "I'm here. I'm not leaving. You take as long as you need to figure out what we mean to you."

A bitter laugh erupted from her. "What we mean to *me*? I know what we mean to me, Daniel. I've known all along what we mean to me. I've been here. Day after day waiting for you to prove all those *plans* weren't just empty promises and pretty words. I know what we mean to me. I don't have a clue what we mean to *you*."

His jaw tensed as he looked around. "Do you know the moment I fell in love with you?"

She shook her head.

"The moment you held up a strainer to try to ward me off."

She laughed softly at the memory. She couldn't stop herself.

"I'd been hiding in that alley watching you because something in you called out to me. I wanted to protect you from the first moment I saw you. My heart was yours before we even met. And every day that I spent here, I loved you more. But I never believed that we could have the life that I wanted until that day I saw you with a baby on your hip."

She inhaled slowly and lowered her face.

"From that moment," he continued, "I knew I had to make this life a reality. I had to make you love me too. To want that life too. And then, by some miracle that I still don't understand, you said you wanted me, and with that happiness came the realization that I wasn't nearly ready to be the man you needed me to be. My past was a demon I had to tackle on my own. You couldn't fight that for me. I had to leave you so I could have you. I fought and I won. Now my fight is to get you back, and I'll go to battle every day until I win. I told you once you were mine, I wasn't going to give you up easily. Maybe to you I'd given up, but I was fighting. For you. For us. I want what I've wanted since the first time I laid eyes on you...a life and a family with you."

She covered her face with her hands as a sob erupted from her. Pulling her to him, he hugged her as he'd done a thousand times—an all-encompassing embrace that made her want to crawl inside him and meld into his warmth and never leave.

"I love you, Jenna," he whispered in her ear. "With every last bit of my dysfunctional heart, I love you."

She leaned back and braced herself for what she was about to do next. "Come with me. I've got something to show you."

sh

Daniel stopped inside Jenna's door. "Wow. This place is completely different."

"Your uncle hasn't stopped coming up with projects to do since you left. It's almost as if he's been keeping an eye on me." She turned to him and cocked a brow.

He smiled, but didn't confess the promise he'd extracted from his uncle before leaving.

A staircase and cutout in the ceiling made her apartment the top two floors of the building instead of just one loft, as it'd been a few months ago. The first floor was still wide open, but consisted of a living space, a dining room, and the kitchen, as well as the bathroom. Her bedroom was no longer down here.

She tossed her keys on the table.

"This is amazing. What made you decide to expand your place instead of renting out the upstairs like you planned?"

She stared at him for what seemed like forever before she started for the stairs. "Follow me."

"Jen, I didn't come here to…"

She scoffed. "Oh, I'm not taking you into my bed. I want to show you something."

She walked down a hallway in what used to be his living room, and then turned through a newly erected doorway and flipped on a light.

Daniel's chest grew so tight he couldn't breathe. This wasn't just a room.

The walls, a soft shade of pink, were adorned with gray elephants and yellow lions. A white crib sat centered along one wall, a rocking chair beside it, and a changing table sat against another.

He turned slowly, his heart thudding as he took in every inch of the space.

No. This wasn't just a room. This was a nursery.

For a baby girl.

A daughter.

Finally he came face to face with Jenna again. She had her lip between her teeth as she did when her nerves kicked into high gear.

"Charlie's been working hard to get this ready in plenty of time. Kara came over and painted just yesterday. I really like it. She did a great job."

He lowered his gaze, not really hearing a word she was saying. The body he'd memorized and dreamed about every single damn night had changed. Not drastically, but the changes were obvious now that he was really looking at her in the light. Her breasts were fuller, her stomach rounder, her hips just slightly wider.

She was pregnant. She was going to be a mother. To a daughter.

He opened his mouth, but he couldn't seem to find the words.

A blush crept up her neck as his gaze made its way back to her face. "If you recall, last we were time together, things happened pretty quickly. Guess what we forgot to use."

"We..." He swallowed as his heart began thundering in his ears. "We're having a baby?"

A half smile touched her lips. "Looks like that three-year plan is pretty much toast."

He stepped to her, staring at her stomach. Pressing his hands to the bump, he laughed softly. "We're having a baby."

She pulled his hands from her body, but held them until he looked into her eyes. "I'm having a baby," she said firmly.

Bile immediately burned up his throat.

She was going to reject him. No. She couldn't. Not now. Not that he didn't deserve her rejection. He'd walked away from her. She'd been here rebuilding the café, planning for the birth of a child—*their* child—without him. He had no right to come back now and expect her to just open her arms to him. But she couldn't turn him away when they were so close to having everything.

"I'll never cut you out of your daughter's life," she said softly. "But I won't allow you to hurt her, either. You're in or you're out, Daniel. None of this leaving for everyone else's benefit bullshit that you just pulled. You're a father or you're not a father. There is no in-between. You will not walk in and out of her life and make her feel like she means nothing to you."

"I'm a father," he said without hesitation.

There was no reason to hesitate. He'd never turn his back on his child. But he didn't blame Jenna for doubting that. It'd take a long time to fully earn her trust again, but he still had her heart. Her eyes betrayed her attempt to be distant. "I'm not going anywhere, Jenna. I'm here. For you, for her. For us."

He reached out and when she didn't pull away, he jerked her into his arms and held her in the way that had always eased his pain.

Only this time he was trying to ease her fears.

"This is what I've been fighting for. This is the future I promised you. I won't turn my back on it. I love you so much."

Finally, she wrapped her arms around his waist and he hugged her even more tightly. Pulling back, she met his teary gaze with one of her own. "I love you, too. And I believe you. I believe that you won't leave again. But you need to know I won't be so forgiving in the future. This is your second chance. If you blow it…"

"I won't." He laughed as his heart filled to the point of overflowing. Putting his hands to her stomach, he shook his head. "How can I love her so much already?"

She covered his hands and laughed softly. "Crazy, huh?"

He nodded. Then a million questions hit him at once. "How are you? Are you okay? Do you need to sit? You've been on your feet all day. Have you hired more help? Is she okay?"

Lifting her hands, she stopped the barrage. "I'm fine. She's fine. I have more help because the café is busy all the time now. Believe it or not, having the place vandalized was the best thing to happen to it. Not only did it give Charlie a chance to do all the updates at once, but people couldn't wait to come in and dine at the scene of a crime. Things really turned around after the reopening."

"Good. That's great. I'm so happy for you."

"The doctor says I can work right up until I choose not to."

He put his hands on her face. "Don't overdo it. I'll help as much as I can. Whatever you need."

"I know you will. Listen, you've convinced me to give you a second chance. My family, on the other hand…"

"Yeah, that's going to take some time. I know."

"But I love you, and God help me, I believe you." She closed her eyes and took a breath. "But you ever leave me again—"

He put his hands to her hips and pulled her to him. "I won't. I swear to you right here and right now, you are never getting rid of me." His heart lifted and he could finally breathe again as he looked into her eyes. He belonged here. He finally belonged with her. He finally deserved her, and he would spend his life proving it to her and anyone else who doubted that.

Stroking her hair back, he pictured the image that had gotten him through the darkest of nights away from her. But he didn't have to pretend anymore. The image was a reality, or would be in a few months. Jenna with their baby on her hip. Jenna smiling at their daughter. Filling his heart and soothing his wounds.

"I'm going to drive you crazy. You know that, don't you? You thought I was protective before, you haven't seen anything yet."

Sliding her arms around his neck, she brushed her nose against his. "I'm counting on that."

The bell over the door indicated someone had walked into O'Connell Realty. Meg forced a welcoming smile as she left her office to greet the visitor. Her smile faded as soon as she saw Aiden brushing snow off his shoulders. This was inevitable. Not just the confrontation with Aiden, but the looky-loos poking their heads from behind various doors.

"I've got this," she announced and, like a bunch of gophers, Dianna, Mallory, and Marcus disappeared back into their offices. Even if they weren't watching, Meg knew their ears would be tuned in.

Aiden gave her an uncertain smile and took more time than necessary to wipe his feet on the carpet. Even if she didn't know him as well as she did, she'd be able to read the signs. He was nervous.

After his feet were thoroughly cleaned, he finally spoke. "I hear you're the best real estate agent in town."

Meg wasn't moved by his smile or his praise. "Oh. And where did you hear this?"

"My cousin's wife. She's quite the fan, apparently."

Meg was still unimpressed and didn't try to act otherwise. "I doubt Mal said I was the best. She usually saves that title for herself."

He laughed softly. She didn't.

"Aiden—" she started.

He cut her off. "I'm looking for a three-bedroom, two bath, finished basement—"

"Aiden."

"Big yard. I've spent the too many years in the city. I want to see green. And I'm thinking about getting a dog so I'd prefer if it were fenced."

"*Stop.*"

He clamped his mouth shut and blinked at her as if he were surprised that she didn't want to play his stupid game. She'd be damned if her fury didn't ease just a bit. He always could make her swoon with just a glance.

She added another brick to the wall around her heart to protect it. She didn't like being cold to him and she didn't want to be cold to him, but letting him in would have been foolish. And if there was one thing Meg was never going to be again, it was foolish. At least where Aiden was concerned. "There are two other agencies in town. Use one of them, okay? If you absolutely have to use O'Connell, then talk to Mallory. I don't want to help you."

If he was trying to hide his disappointment, he wasn't doing a very good job. "Okay. But if you aren't busy, do you think we could…"

He left the rest of his statement unspoken. She wanted to scream at him. He always did that. He always left things unsaid and she'd say them for him and he somehow thought that counted. It didn't count. Unspoken words didn't count. Not anymore.

"What?" She refused to even consider budging until he said what he meant.

"Talk. About us. How things ended. Where we go from here."

"I'm at work."

"Maybe I can steal you away for an early lunch? Or a coffee break?"

She wanted to refuse him. But if she didn't settle this now, she was never going to get anything done. She'd replay this conversation. She'd replay every moment she'd ever spent with him and every moment she'd spent missing him until she lost her freaking mind. The only way to break that cycle before it started was to deal with him now.

She frowned, certain she was going to regret this. "Let me get my things." After grabbing her coat and purse, she leaned into Marcus's office. "I'll be back."

"Take your time," he said.

She hadn't doubted the entire office knew the situation, but the paternal concern in his voice confirmed it. "Thanks." She didn't say anything to Aiden as they left the warmth of the office and marched toward her car.

Aiden matched her rushed stride. "A lot has changed since I left. Some of the places I loved are gone. Stonehill Café has had a complete remodel."

"Yes, I know." She slammed her car door harder than was necessary before shoving her key into the ignition. The café was within walking distance, but she wasn't wearing the right shoes or the right attitude to go that far with Aiden at her side. She'd be too tempted to jerk off her brand-new Kenneth Cole sandal and shove the heel through his eye.

"But the town still feels the same," he said from her passenger seat, "like nothing has changed at all. It's strange. Like living in some alternate universe."

She didn't respond. Nothing that came to her mind was nice. Maybe if he hadn't left, he would have been here when the café was vandalized and remodeled. Maybe if he hadn't left, he wouldn't feel so strange being here now. Silence fell between them as she drove. His discomfort was as obvious as her anger.

He cleared his throat. "It's great that Mallory and Phil are having a baby, huh?"

She smiled a genuine smile for the first time since he'd suddenly appeared back in her life. "Yes. It's wonderful."

"Do you know what they're having?"

"They want to be surprised. I can't imagine not knowing," Meg said. "It would drive me crazy."

Aiden laughed. "You always did have to plan ahead. You take Type A to the next level."

Her smile fell as she glanced over at him. He appeared to realize his misstep and opened his mouth but didn't correct himself. She didn't correct him either, mostly because he was right. Meg didn't like surprises. Ever. Not even good ones. But he had lost the right to point out her flaws a long time ago.

ALSO BY MARCI BOLDEN

STONEHILL SERIES:

The Road Leads Back

Friends Without Benefits

The Forgotten Path

Jessica's Wish

This Old Café

Forever Yours (coming soon)

OTHER TITLES:

Unforgettable You (coming soon)

A Life Without Water (coming soon)

ABOUT THE AUTHOR

As a teen, Marci Bolden skipped over young adult books and jumped right into reading romance novels. She never left.

Marci lives in the Midwest with her husband, kiddos, and numerous rescue pets. If she had an ounce of willpower, Marci would embrace healthy living, but until cupcakes and wine are no longer available at the local market, she will appease her guilt by reading self-help books and promising to join a gym "soon."

Visit her here:
www.marcibolden.com

facebook.com/MarciBoldenAuthor
twitter.com/BoldenMarci
instagram.com/marciboldenauthor